Austeja Sciavinskaite

Clara Drummond

ROLE PLAY

Translated from the Portuguese by Daniel Hahn

Clara Drummond is a Brazilian writer and journalist based in Lisbon. Her work has appeared in *Vogue, Elle, Harper's Bazaar,* and *Marie Claire. Role Play* is her third novel.

Daniel Hahn is a writer, an editor, and a translator, with about a hundred books to his name. Recent books include *Catching Fire: A Translation Diary* and translations of novels from Angola, Venezuela, and Guatemala. He is currently writing a book about Shakespeare and translation, and coediting a collection of Brazilian short stories.

ROLE PLAY

ROLE PLAY

CLARA DRUMMOND

*Translated from the Portuguese
by Daniel Hahn*

FSG Originals
Farrar, Straus and Giroux
New York

FSG Originals
Farrar, Straus and Giroux
120 Broadway, New York 10271

Copyright © 2022 by Clara Drummond
Published by arrangement with Redondo Books
International Literary Agency
Translation copyright © 2024 by Daniel Hahn
All rights reserved
Printed in the United States of America
Originally published in Portuguese in 2022 by Companhia
das Letras, Brazil, as *Os coadjuvantes*
English translation published in the United States by
Farrar, Straus and Giroux
First American edition, 2024

Library of Congress Cataloging-in-Publication Data
Names: Drummond, Clara, 1986– author. | Hahn, Daniel, translator.
Title: Role play / Clara Drummond ; translated from the Portuguese
by Daniel Hahn.
Other titles: Coadjuvantes. English
Description: First American edition. | New York : FSG Originals,
Farrar, Straus and Giroux, 2024. |
Identifiers: LCCN 2023050710 | ISBN 9780374611286 (paperback)
Subjects: LCGFT: Novels.
Classification: LCC PQ9698.414.R86 C6313 2024 | DDC 869.3/5—
dc23/eng/20231214
LC record available at https://lccn.loc.gov/2023050710

Designed by Patrice Sheridan

Our books may be purchased in bulk for promotional, educational,
or business use. Please contact your local bookseller or the Macmillan
Corporate and Premium Sales Department at 1-800-221-7945, extension
5442, or by email at MacmillanSpecialMarkets@macmillan.com.

www.fsgoriginals.com • www.fsgbooks.com
Follow us on social media at @fsgoriginals and @fsgbooks

1 3 5 7 9 10 8 6 4 2

For Claudinho

Now I am quietly waiting for
the catastrophe of my personality
to seem beautiful again,
and interesting, and modern.

—FRANK O'HARA

ROLE PLAY

1

I'm a misandrist and a misogynist, I've got no patience
for men or for women—I mean, nothing against them,
as they say, I just don't want anything to do with them, I
never have anything to talk about, and I feel constantly
like I'm being patronizing, either that or it's them patronizing me. But I'm not a misanthrope, 'cause I do
like gay men. They're the one type of human you can
properly get along with as equals. I just don't feel comfortable in the milieu I got assigned to at birth. Just the
thought of marriage and kids, the whole thing makes me
want to puke. Biology is not destiny. Right here I could
reel off all the reasons I've come to that conclusion, but
it would sound dumb, and dated, and most of all I'd
set myself up right off the bat looking like one of those
idiot girls who just want a gay best friend of their very
own. Gays aren't pets. Seriously, get with it. And so, just
to be clear I'm not one of *those* women, I'll drop a word

in Pajubá—intermediate level ideally, 'cause the basic words even my mom would know and advanced vocabulary would look like I'm trying way too hard. Either that or I'll decide to tell some meaningful story, kind of like that time two of my friends who didn't know each other were fucking in one of the Berghain darkrooms. Hey, aren't you a friend of Vivian's? one of them asked, I don't know what stage they'd gotten to at the time. It's good being part of a group. But whatever, I've got to get a grip on my anxiety, not go firing off these coded messages, sometimes even in the first few minutes of a conversation, 'cause a person who belongs is chill, they're not making any effort to project an image, they just feel at home, and I really want to feel at home.

For a long time, I was living between Rio and São Paulo, depending on the job, sometimes permanent, sometimes temporary, always erratic, unstable, badly paid, when it was paid at all. But I'd put myself through it anyway, since each one of those experiences would represent gold stars on my résumé. I'm a freelance curator, I've worked in galleries, biennials, museums, studios, I've assisted on major exhibitions, been sole producer of smaller but significant shows, I write art crit for magazines and newspapers, here as well as abroad. And then people congratulate me, my parents give me some gift or other, like a trip to Berlin, a Comme des Garçons wallet, a Francesca Woodman photograph. I don't work with painters, or photographers, because they're straight, and every now and then the whole thing totally goes to shit, even if some of them can be charming, with that typical artist's self-confidence. And before I know it I'm fucking the guy at the opening of his exhibition, locked in the gallery restroom, sharing a line from the night before, at eleven on a Saturday morning. When it's over, they always emerge even more self-confident, after a quickie with a girl ten years younger, and I almost never come. Which is why I always preferred other kinds of artists, who, sure, they might also be narcissists, but at least they're fun, so they don't bring along any risk of emotional mishaps.

When my thirtieth birthday was coming up, my parents bought me an apartment in Botafogo, two bedrooms, hardwood floors, ninety square meters, twenty-four-hour doorman. And as a bonus, they also lent me a Sergio Rodrigues 'Mole' armchair (the dog had chewed some of the leather, they were supposed to take it back when they found a good upholsterer, but I think they've forgotten, it's already been two years now). It looked good next to that huge João Silva photograph. That was a gift—I mean, I paid for the printing and the frame, but now my house has one more work of art, and it's from the same series they've got at MALBA. That period coincided with an upgrade of my résumé. From then on, the one single criterion for choosing jobs was how they contributed to my career, disregarding any financial considerations. And if the budget got a bit squeezed, whatever that meant, well, I'd just rent out the apartment for a couple weeks and hang in my family's spare apartment down in São Paulo. This plan was especially lucrative during Carnaval and New Year's. That way, I got money for several months, which would allow me a break for a vacation, perhaps taking a course abroad, and, I dunno, maybe some Botox.

The apartment was perfectly located, it had vendors out on the street 24-7, always well stocked up with Heinekens. Darlene, whose spot was right in front of my place, told me the other side of the road was dangerous, there's even been an execution, she said, grim business. I didn't worry, I reckoned maybe she was just trying to scare off the competition. Having your own place is such an utter joy, I get to choose the color of the bedroom wallpaper, I turn what used to be the maid's room into a spacious closet, I've got a kitchen just off the living room, noise-proof windows. I wanted to leave the bathroom almost identical to how it was originally 'cause I do love that aesthetic, that whole 1950s middle-class vibe. I don't understand this universe of yours, with apartments just kind of appearing out of nowhere, said Marina Falcão. Every week we'd improvise some little party, I'd supply the fridge, the bags of ice, the speaker, the red light bulb, and everyone would bring their own drinks, their own drugs, their playlists of choice. The elderly neighbors would complain sometimes, but no biggie, like Alex used to say: They'll be dead soon enough . . . either that, or they'll have been gentrified out. Alex was responsible for bringing along the new generation of alt nightlife queers, every one of them so proud of their little acts of subversion, their colorful earrings, pink fingernails, maybe a distinctly feminine outfit, something I approve of and encourage. It makes the cast more diverse, it enriches the ambience.

That day, I'd organized a dinner here at home for my closest friends, after which we'd be going to a rave where Rodrigo was DJing. I was so glad he'd come out, including to his family, who were even more conservative than mine and who'd previously had high hopes we'd get married. A few years ago, he actually proposed that we start a fake relationship just so his parents would give him a break. And as a bonus, we'd get an awesome party and the use of their place in Paris. The possibility of a conventional heteronormative life did even seem a bit tempting then, for like fifteen minutes, but no more than that. In my opinion, Rodrigo should have dumped his school friends, those idiots who worked in finance, to meet more interesting people in the art world.

Rodrigo's set was going to be the last of the night, not till morning, so we left home around two. The rave wasn't in some dark, noisy little dive, with lasers, strobe lights, projections—it was free entry, in a square close to the Banco do Brasil Cultural Center. In reality the square was a kind of public courtyard with a fence and only one way in, with two security guards to make sure the numbers stayed under control, hand out bracelets, and keep an eye out for trouble. A specific niche, the wealthy gay crowd, mostly white, who despise traditional symbols of ostentation and are allied to progressive, liberal values, not necessarily those of the left, at least not in economic terms. As usual, there were vendors selling drinks outside the rave while people waited to get in.

To my surprise, Darlene, the vendor from my street, was there, though not selling beers, but caipirinhas. Next to her, a bad-tempered old man was selling Heinekens. I gave her a wave, smiling, and shouted: Hi! João Silva left our spot to give her a hug, kiss her cheek, ask about her son. He could do shit like that without sounding patronizing; I couldn't. Which was why I preferred to be more discreet, maintain a more professional relationship, customer and vendor, scared I might say something stupid. And maybe 'cause in my head she worked outside my house every day, I hadn't even noticed that on Saturdays she was somewhere else, she was someone else. And I certainly didn't know anything about Darlene's family. The line shuffled forward a few meters, but soon stalled, leaving us level with her

mobile caipirinha stall. I thought you might be here!
João Silva said. What the hell, João Silva lived in São
Paulo, how come he knew Darlene's professional itin-
erary? All this just from the times he'd been downstairs
to buy beers at those parties at my place? It was taking forever to get in. Forty minutes without moving.
Still, whatever, we were kept distracted, chatting with
Darlene. She remembered details from before, asked
about how earlier events had unfolded. She was smart,
quick, funny, clued-in, even kinda cultured; she spoke
our language, she wasn't evangelical, she voted PSOL.
The conversation was so enjoyable, nobody noticed the
sudden arrival of the municipal police.

At first, nobody was too stressed about it, they were
always harmless enough, but we were at a point in Brazilian politics when things were starting to get weird.
The police van that appeared in front of us was not
much different from those used by the more imposing,
BOPE-style special squads. Five men with puffed-up
chests positioned themselves in front of the line, radiat-
ing a hostility that was emphasized by their nightsticks,
which were larger than usual. First they tackled the bad-
tempered old man, taking all his beers, putting them in
the back of the van. Hey, that's stealing! yelled Marina
Falcão, and the rest of the line agreed, with jeering so
intense it muffled the sound of Italo disco from inside.
This didn't seem to hold the police officers back. On

the contrary, it seemed to considerably increase their fervor, and they started to advance on Darlene real aggressively. Her cocktail-making gear got smashed up, along with her bottles of cachaça, which were tossed onto the ground. Darlene shouted and tried to extricate herself from the grip of the man holding her arm, and in retaliation received a whack from a nightstick. Alex tried to intervene, to put his body between them, with his earrings, his painted nails, his purple eye shadow, and he also took some blows, on his leg, his arm, and when he tried to retreat to us, his ribs. He wasn't the only partygoer to take a stand, but the beating was directed only at him. In all the commotion, somebody threw a canister of tear gas at the feet of the people in the line, a meter away from the municipal police.

The security guards working the rave rushed everyone inside. Only the vendors were left on the street. Maybe the cops were intimidated by the idea of going into a party for the elites, it could have been for their own protection. It never even crossed our minds that the vendors might have been there to attend the rave themselves. In theory it was a free event, and there was no reason they should have stayed outside, especially because, by that point, their drinks had been confiscated. But there was a mutual understanding, silent and unanimous, that they did not belong in that setting, and that was all.

Alex went home, slightly injured but okay, and the rest of us stayed at the rave through dawn, since the acid had already started to take effect. Forget about it, Vivian, said Marina Falcão. But the moment I'd gone in, I knew something serious was still happening outside. I tried, unsuccessfully, to make my way back through the people who were crowding in. The protective railings, along with my poor eyesight, worsened by the tear gas, obscured my view. A shape was writhing, struggling to move, nearly on the opposite corner. I sensed it might be Darlene. Had she been beaten extra violently in those ten minutes of confusion when everyone—that is, all of us, the usual partygoers—was pouring into the square? Or was it just some tramp, a street kid, a crackhead? Maybe. Ten minutes is long enough for one hell of a beating. But if it was Darlene, somebody in the line would surely have yelled, would have protested, and not just followed my steps in toward the Italo disco beats.

2

We were a group of twenty friends, if not more, some genuinely talented, others in vaguely creative professions, all successful, all photogenic, all kinda nice-looking if not extremely nice-looking, which is something that matters to me. The most significant among them, at least in my life, were João Silva, Alex, Marina Falcão, and now Rodrigo. I might not be the best art curator, but I know for sure I'm the best curator of people. That's my proudest work. It's allowed me to create the life path I've always wanted. Sometimes when we're all together I feel like I'm the main character in an imaginary movie that takes place over the course of a single night. The blue and red lights on the dance floor, which we often re-create in our homes, reduce our physical defects and highlight our best qualities, and we can pretend we are perfect. But sometimes my morning-after memory retains only those scenes I'd rather discard: all my excessive effort shows through, like an actress who never disappears into her part, too worried about getting recognition for her performance, and that's pathetic. I'd love to be naturally the person I seem to be.

The other day, at the end of an after-party, I think it was Monday, I was chatting with one of those friends, finishing a few leftover lines on the dining table while watching the morning sun gain in strength. Both of us wearing shades, smoking at the window, my red lipstick still solid, my black lace bra acting as a bikini top, silk blouse hanging from the bookcase, high-waisted pants hiding the bit of flab on my stomach, which wasn't exactly photogenic in that brightness. Over the course of the night, we'd gone downstairs at least three times to buy beers, this time on the other side of the street. Having an after-party on a weekday is super classy, I always think it's subversive, anti-capitalist. Or maybe it's an aristocratic habit, something only the rich do, I couldn't say, maybe somewhere between the two? Alex was in the study, deep in a spanking session with the door wide open, I couldn't even go to the bathroom down the hall for fear of glimpsing his upturned little butt. Might have been, I dunno, some artist friend of João Silva's, maybe? I couldn't even keep up a conversation with the one remaining guest who still had half a bag of cocaine, 'cause every few words we'd hear this

"Pam! Pam! Pam!" like somebody was punctuating our sentences. In those days, some variation of that scenario was a frequent occurrence, in the pantry, in the utility area, in the maid's room, on the living-room sofa, to the point that it started irritating me, since I'd only just moved in and hadn't even had my own first go on the bed with anybody, and there was Alex, scoring more sexual partners than me.

For the first two years, I kept myself busy exclusively with Luiz Felipe: engineer, pothead, surfer, vegan. A Copacabana boy, angelic face, who meditates every morning, dreams of traveling around the world, selling his car, going everywhere by bicycle, public transport at most. He's not the most attractive man I've ever had sex with, he's kinda dumb, charmless. His good looks are standard, they're sort of Rio Classic, the type you find by the dozen on the beaches, tanned, curly blond hair, blue eyes, with the naive self-confidence of someone who was the best-looking boy in school but didn't know how to, or chose not to, make the most of it. Luiz Felipe is unpretentious—he quotes self-help books with Eastern leanings, sometimes he'll give me one as a gift and believe me when I tell him I loved it, when in reality I mock his literary repertoire behind his back, reading bits aloud to entertain guests, laughing through the early hours at his superstitions, then snorting coke off the cover of a Deepak Chopra. But one way or another, that philosophy must have some effect, 'cause there's a kind of wisdom in that boy I can't pin down.

On the sofa at my place, before I unbutton his pants, during our standard five-minute chat, he would confess his overburdened conscience, how all he wanted was to contribute to the world, do something positive. But if he quit his job for some more altruistic venture, without his salary from the construction firm, he wouldn't then be able to realize his dream of surfing in Australia. I would kiss him, hold his dick, shut him up. He does have the most beautiful body in the world, just well-defined enough, strong but lean. The message I wrote after our first meeting was: *This is Vivian, from last Saturday. I've got a bottle of wine at home and four hours to fuck.* Luiz Felipe answered yes, asked my address, the time, no hesitation. He's different from the others, he doesn't call me beautiful, only hot, or sometimes "you little slut." I like it, I find it just sweet enough, even affectionate, sort of tender, kind of adorable. Is it possible that I fell in love with a guy with such a dull profile just because he slapped me, because he spat on me while we fucked and happened to have a special talent for fisting? I always said my greatest fear was to end up married to an investment banker, but a civil engineer might actually be worse, it's just so generic. The first time we fucked, I cried in my cab home, 5 a.m., after seven uninterrupted hours of sex. It was almost romantic, the city lights at night, the back seat of the car, my recent memories, the whole sense of novelty, like something special had happened that might not happen again, and there was Roxette playing, or it could have been some other band but let's pretend it was Roxette. Statistics show it's normal for a woman not to experience orgasm till age thirty, and I'm fine with that, I'm not frigid, repressed, someone who's just in desperate need of a proper fuck. Luiz Felipe says I'm the only girl who doesn't get scandalized by his fantasies, but I'm not sure I believe him. I'd be waiting for him all week, like a nice monogamous girl, while he must be out dancing forró, kissing some basic girls with no personality, with their mundane chatter, their tacky little blouses, standard-issue femininity, probably totally square in bed, conventional as their ordinary appearance, or at least that's what I'd like to think.

Luiz Felipe said that one time he'd invited a buddy of his to join him in fucking his then girlfriend and they double-penetrated her. The idea turned me on, but he didn't feel comfortable about fucking again with another guy around. So I had to content myself with having a vibrator in the role of the extra element. It wasn't as thrilling as I expected. Still, over the course of our encounters, we went on doing it, maybe in the hope that it might, at a certain point, suddenly become spectacular. Except that one day, instead of an orgasm, I had to deal with getting the vibrator stuck inside my anus. My first attempt to retrieve it ended up making things worse, and I thought, ugh, I'm so fucked now, it's going into my gut. I couldn't stop thinking about Sylvia Plath. The character in my favorite book has this hemorrhage when she loses her virginity. She needs to go to the hospital with the boy, who's a stranger. It was the fifties, I explained, scared I might suffer the same fate, but he'd never heard of Sylvia Plath. Finally, after around fifteen minutes of contorting, me trying to reach for the vibrator up my ass, while he was pushing on it from inside my vagina, it all worked out, I didn't need to go to the hospital, and we went back to fucking.

I was sure I'd never see Luiz Felipe again after that. There was a three-week hiatus between the double-penetration incident and our next contact—it was horrible, I got anxious, I felt guilty. It was the only time he didn't message to ask if I'd gotten home okay. Maybe the most important things in a relationship are horniness, respect, and affection, along with communication that's clear, light, and effortless. I think other people's opinion is secondary next to what happens à deux. I was even missing the white porcelain floor of his little apartment on Rua Constante Ramos. But Luiz Felipe had only gone away to visit with his grandparents in the interior of Minas Gerais. When I told him about my paranoia, he laughed and said something like: What BS!

Our weekly encounters, which became ever more surprising and exuberant, somehow managed to relax my normally rigid judgments and make me pay attention to what he said. Luiz Felipe gave no signs that might make me consider him an intelligent guy. Which is why it was a surprise whenever I did get to see him as kind of sensitive and observant. Our exchanges, even the most existential, almost philosophical ones, were more fluid than those with the photographer whose work I admired, or with the screenwriter of my favorite movie, both of them failed relationships, in sexual as well as emotional terms. I liked the idea of being with those men, that was the sort of couple I imagined for myself. Except that when it happened, it wasn't actually all that cool, I got mistreated. With Luiz Felipe, the whole thing was good, the chat, the kissing, the sex, the spooning. Even the morning after, which was always an awkward moment with other guys, was lovely—he'd make breakfast, the best green juice in the world, then head out to surf while I got a few more hours of sleep.

Luiz Felipe knows he's the best sex of my life, that I'd never come so intensely, that my exes were selfish in bed as in life, and he can't get why I stayed with them. Luiz Felipe said if the best thing about those guys was their photos or their movies, wouldn't it be smarter just to keep those, the way you do with other artists who are already dead, or like, living in some other country? I felt so adolescent when he said this, you idiot, idiot, idiot. This isn't the best sex of my life because you call me a little slut, or because of the orgasms, I told him. It's the best sex of my life because it's like I'm returning home—not to the home where I grew up, with all its rigid rules, but to another home, beyond my unconscious, like I'm returning to a place I truly belong, a place where I was before being born. Luiz Felipe hugged me, kissed me, we had sex one more time, and I experienced that same feeling again, even more powerfully.

Maybe being so totally dazzled sexually was affecting my cognitive judgment, not least because every conversation happened in gaps between the sex, the two of us naked in bed, our bodies intertwined. Marina Falcão would say I was in love, but there was something mocking in her diagnosis, which put me on the defensive, and I'd reply, Impossible—he doesn't even have any proper books in his house, and he only watches the big blockbusters. Luiz Felipe would have nothing to talk about with my friends—I mean, can you even imagine? If they were talking about the Anthropocene, he'd reply with something about reusable shopping bags, and straws, and bicycles. But you don't stop smiling, Marina Falcão insisted. Maybe I really am so far gone that I don't even give a crap about Alex's comments about him: So he's some kind of right-wing environmentalist? Girl, I think that might be even worse than being a right-wing queer. And yeah, Alex is correct, I have no idea what role this kid will play in my life, and maybe just getting a good fucking from a good-hearted boy isn't enough? It's just, I'm too insecure not to be super-ficial, I need to cling on to any material things I can, which serve as my points of reference, this is me, this is my world, these are the laws that guide me and those around me. If I think about feelings and sensations and immaterial things, I'll be lost, adrift. Life without a handrail seems as mysterious to me, as inconceivable, as life in outer space, or life after death, or whatever we were before we were born. Luiz Felipe and I reached a point where even the tiniest contact between our skins produced a small ecstasy, reminding me of my adoles-cent loves, when the most erotic thing of all was that chance contact, skin to skin when handing over a book, a pencil, a workbook, a scarf, opening up a whole uni-verse of senses; the memory of my last orgasm the week before got all muddled up with that memory from ad-olescence, part rejection, part discovery, part passion. Even after weeks, months, almost a year, he only has to touch me, and I guide his hand to where I want it, I feel pleasure instantly, and I can't help thinking there's something to it that's more than physical. The next day, I push away this flow of memory, tell myself it's just sex. Love doesn't happen in a vacuum, in a bedroom, it's not only those one-on-one moments, in the privacy of the home, which start out seeming so very precious, with such a strong emotional charge, but end up getting rarer, drowning in banality, or, at best, mere nostalgia. Love is also in the world, and Luiz Felipe doesn't belong to my world, ergo, this must not be love.

3

My family has: an apartment just off Ipanema beach, partial view, 400 square meters, which is where the live-in maid works, and the cleaner who comes Tuesdays and Thursdays, and the driver who drives my mother's car, which is armored, naturally; a country house, with 10,000 square meters of property, 300 of built area, indoor and outdoor pools, maid on the weekends, gardener every day, and another car there, a more basic one, for taking the dogs; a beach house, 800 square meters of property, 150 of built area, with no pool or maid or permanent gardener 'cause it only gets used in the summer; and a pied-à-terre in São Paulo. None of it's huge, really; you can't have everything, you got to make the numbers work, not spend too much, since after all, as I was taught, we're only in the middle class. Still, even on a limited budget, some design pieces and works of art do make up part of the décor, along with other bits of furniture bought while traveling or in cities in the interior, from local artisans. The result is so much more charming than most of the houses of friends and acquaintances, much more overbearing places where I would always go in my childhood, and where the rest of the family goes still.

Over the last ten years, our income's reduced substantially. It used to be that everybody traveled business, including the nanny, when my sister and I were little; now it's only Dad and Mom. The hotels have lost a star, from five down to four. Six months ago, the big Amílcar de Castro in the dining room went up for auction. The Di Cavalcanti from the library's going to meet the same fate. Both will get replaced by some contemporary photograph that I get to choose, something in the five-thousand-dollar range, and I'll get a commission. I suggested renting out the beach house, a monthly contract would be less of a worry for them, or alternatively, if they wanted to keep spending time there over the summer, like they usually do already, they could stick it on Airbnb? And as a bonus, it'll bring in a little extra cash. Maria Elisa, my mother, changed the subject the moment she heard the phrase "a little extra cash." Oh, can you even imagine! Total strangers having access to our personal belongings, bedsheets, books, face creams! Absolutely no need. We're middle class, but not *that* middle class.

Maria Elisa is more scared of waking up suddenly penniless than the manicurist who does our nails. She's always complaining, saying how expensive things have gotten, gas prices, goat cheese, Pilates, my analyst. The other day, it was repairing the washing machine: It's outrageous, I'll need to get some other quotes, this fellow is terribly pricey, I'm sure he's overcharging me, I'm going to ask him to give me a discount, it's out of the question . . . The electrician, who is the doorman's brother and who provides his services to other residents of the building, agreed to do the job for half the price. The following week, the house was filled with waiters organizing serving dishes, filled with moqueca, ravioli, roast beef—enough food for all forty guests, including a candidate for governor, currently riding high in the polls. Seen from outside, you'd think the money had just appeared out of nowhere, all of a sudden, dozens of bottles of wine, white and red, and many more of rosé, the miracle at Cana. The negotiations over the washing machine repair had not been a matter of saving money per se, it was a sport, a hobby even, a bet with herself, so much so that Mom's always saying, proudly: Oh, I can always get a great bargain! On the day of the lunch for all those guests, the electrician had come to fix something or other at a neighbor's apartment. He saw all the coming and going—I got embarrassed, but not Mom.

Money can seem like it's a concrete thing: the

supermarket shop, rent, tax, transport, tickets, bank account, ATM, but really, it's very abstract. It's an even bigger taboo than death or sex. In that environment, being poor is a worse sin than going to prison, according to my friend Rodrigo. His father was involved in a corruption scandal when we were kids. He was convicted of some kind of fraud involving savings bonds and spent a few years out of the country until eventually the charge lapsed. And still, no trace of any ostracism, he went on getting invited, being greatly liked, welcome, a member of the country club. Everybody wanted to stay in his hôtel particulier in the 16ème. He wasn't considered a crook among his peers because he came from a good family. It's kind of distressing knowing that those sorts of people were often at my house, and not just one of them, or two, but several, all with the same profile. Is Dad a lobbyist? I asked my mom once, and she promptly replied: Oh, Vivian, *everybody* here lobbies, even me.

My dad, Sérgio, is VP of the biggest security and surveillance firm in the country. Before that, he had other roles, both public and private sector, in banks, insurance, oil companies, phone companies, mining, transportation. His hiring almost always came about through his friendship with the company's owner, with the mayor, with the minister, or with somebody obscurer, someone operating behind the scenes. Rodrigo says everyone from that generation built their life on patrimonialism. It was almost second nature, a way of life, the only way they knew how to relate—it had nothing to do with ethics or morality. And it wasn't that his friends all got caught up in those maneuverings like misappropriation of funds, kickbacks in suitcases, dollar bills hidden in your underwear. Honestly, things like that are actually kind of tacky, there are plenty more sophisticated mechanisms for getting rich, which are more discreet or even legal—imagine that!—not involving any official transgression. You've always got the option of passing some legislative rider in Congress. No reason to break the law if you have the power to change the law. Just one meeting with the president or a minister, and a provisional measure can be arranged. Sometimes, they aren't thieves per se, but some whole other category, as if foul play got purified through bureaucracy, like the Eucharist, or dialysis. To tell the truth, I don't understand much about it, and I was forbidden from broaching the subject with my parents. Like Sérgio says, asking friends about their rap sheets isn't polite.

Ana Amélia Noronha, my grandmother, was the kind of rich old lady character you'd get on a TV soap, except not actually rich. She used to be ambassador to Vienna, so it didn't matter, she still fit the part. There is no tourism lower budget than sleeping and eating as a guest of the right friends in the leading capitals of Europe. It's through those accumulated savings that symbolic capital materializes in the physical world. Sometimes, the stay can be existentially better than a good hotel, as it comes coupled with social events, where there are more potential friends, potential offers of accommodation, all of which helps to form a personality that's interesting, experienced, cosmopolitan. The grand-monde parties my grandparents frequented seventy years ago make up part of the family mythology. It's always the right time for remembering the old days. They were there, mere extras in scenes that, I'm pretty sure, only seldom made the final cut, but still, that attachment to those yellowing magazines, kept in the study closet, assured their self-importance, as if a succession of small victories could lead to something that ennobled the soul.

At the start of the twentieth century, my family genuinely was very rich, the owner of a chain of department stores that ended up going bankrupt in the '60s. In those days, Ana Amélia had her collection of haute couture dresses and frequented Dener's atelier, and Clodovil's. On their trips to Paris, they would typically book a whole floor of the George V. I remember hearing them sigh when recalling the hotel, which they called their "second home." The money went away when Dad was coming out of adolescence; it took a few years more for him to realize he was mortal, that he needed to work for a living. Ana Amélia managed to keep up appearances with the selection of jewels and dresses that did not get put up for auction and with her privileged position at Foreign Affairs. Life went on quite comfortably for everybody—the spacious apartments, weekend homes, traveling twice a year, servants, the whole bit. Her seven children all lived reasonably well, or extremely well in the case of the firstborn, who supports his younger brother and has an island in Angra dos Reis. Still, the opulence of the past was kept as a reminder. Rodrigo said the people from the club are always commenting: Oh, the Noronhas have lost all their money. My whole life I've been surrounded by the ex-rich, or by those people who hang around the genuinely rich, I'm talking about the private-plane rich, not the normal business-class rich. In the case of my family, the two categories overlap, creating a sense of inferiority that is very specific, kind of comic and also kinda sad.

In financial terms, Dad wasn't able to stand out from his peers, managed to acquire only the elementary kit, so he had to find another strategy, invent a compensatory narrative, like the overvaluing of notable ancestors, these tropical pseudoaristocrats who'd been reincarnated in the names of streets and avenues. Tradition was just something inherently moral, and kind of adorable? It's so awkward when one of my friends just happens to meet my dad and he asks their family name, then tries to make the link to some acquaintance of his or a historical figure. Really sort of amazing he never realized how impolite that was, even rude. When I was a teenager, when I had girlfriends who were dumber, and heterosexual all the way down to their toes, they'd smile awkwardly, ashamed, and just quietly murmur: No. That is, until the other day, when Alex, sort of fed up, replied that his grandparents were illiterate and so, no, they were *not* the São Paulo Mesquitas.

My grandparents' photo album has hardly any pictures of their young kids, at birthdays or graduations, only portraits of themselves with heads of state, kings and queens, bishops and popes. The Noronhas have been diplomats for generations, almost always ambassadors, if not ministers. Or, as Dad likes to say, members of the Kennel Club. This professional tradition means my family is considered intellectual compared to our peers, not that that's saying much. Before she died, my grandmother set up a social media account, where she published these indirect little moral lessons: *Money is no use without culture. Please note: you ought not to write "you shouldn't of." The proper way to write it is: "you shouldn't have."* I wanted to correct her, to point out that it really didn't matter, but if I did this in public, in the comment box under the post itself, I risked getting cut out of her will.

When Ana Amélia died, age eighty-five, she left only hospital bills and an apartment on Avenida Atlântica (500 square meters, looking straight out over Copacabana beach, marble entrance hall, no garage, whorehouse on the corner, muggings on the sidewalk, a crappy restaurant in the courtyard with live music, plastic menus, McCain fries). I felt jealousy at the painless death, anxiety at the thought of such a long life, relief to not have to do any more Sunday lunches at her house with the Catholic cousins. But I thought it only polite to fake a bit of sadness just out of sensitivity to the rest of the family. I did the whole performance, even skipping the opening of João Silva's solo show at MAM. At the burial, Dad said philosophically: My mother always said that death is like the sun. You can't look directly at either one of them. I kept my mouth shut, not wanting to correct him, to point out that Grandma did not come up with the line, that it came from her bedside book, a collection of supposedly literary quotations. Ah, Ana Amélia was always so very wise, replied one old man, an ex-minister from the military dictatorship.

Maria Elisa didn't think much of her, but still she was in shock, like it wasn't natural, like it wasn't time, like it was all a huge surprise, like she had never wished for her death, never thought about death, not even in the abstract. Whenever somebody dies, that's what it's like, an upset, a great blow, which is weird, seeing as everybody dies. People spend so much time worried about le placement for a dinner seating that there's no time left to think about death. Maybe that's why placements exist. We're all so preoccupied with gaining points, climbing the ladder, getting as close as we can to the top, but the end of the road is death, and that is obvious, but isn't. It's hard to memorize the correct rules for a placement, because it's through them that we go up more steps, and if it was easy, well, then everyone would get to go up, and where'd be the fun in that? The mobility's got to be stopped—we need to preserve things the way they were, reinforce the hereditary meritocracy. It's no use being dedicated if you don't know the language, the pronunciation, the accent. Upward mobility works like a board game full of arbitrary rules that should provide entertainment but produce only boredom.

Even now, there are rigid financial punishments whenever I insist on escaping from a given set of rules, like I was just some employee, only with a monthly allowance instead of a wage, and with the allowance comes the expectation that one day I will shape myself to those parameters. Maria Elisa makes the rules quite clear by email whenever there's a family dinner scheduled: Vivian, you know it's in your own best interest if you behave diplomatically, no talking politics, especially with your cousin, you know she doesn't think like you. Ana Cândida, the cousin—Catholic, monarchist, hugely fat—was the late-arriving only child of my father's brother, who is a partner in a construction firm and, therefore, is not middle class, as he's even got a plane. Now thirty, Ana Cândida has never worked, except maybe one of those pretend little jobs at most. I don't think she's even got a degree—she's waiting for a good match, someone who will follow the strict rules laid down by Ana Amélia Noronha. It's like arranged marriages hadn't been abolished, they'd just changed configuration, become more lenient, inclusive, while still limited to a few dozen viable candidates. None of this choosing to marry for love or money, that's so vulgar. All you need is a bit of curating of the partnership, then it's inevitable that the throes of passion will happen with somebody suitable, presentable, good-looking. The match should be someone who can accompany her as an equal, not just as a consort. Ana Cândida doesn't know that money isn't enough, that she'll also have to lose weight, otherwise the criteria will need changing. My aunt, who's plump too, says, To be with you, my child, oh, it'd be like winning the lottery! And the girl believes it, her ego inflated by her mother's friends, who write *lovely!*, *gorgeous!*, *a vision!* on all the selfies she posts on Insta.

Over the last year, Ana Cândida has tried to get closer to me again—she's been to electronic music parties, she's even got herself a gay friend, a social-climbing would-be stylist, whom she takes on family holidays.

My theory is that she needs a total revamp, since she hasn't managed to land a husband yet: she needs to try out a different wardrobe, go for something more modern, so she doesn't get seen as a failure. But she can't do it, she doesn't understand the codes, she's actually really dumb. On social media she looks like she's in some costume, with these totally dated signs of wealth, it's like the opera, black-tie parties, chalets in the snow, St. Barts. The plane, naturally, plays the starring role, the stage for all her selfies. I always think: Ugh, how tacky, she learned nothing from Grandma. Maybe she doesn't have ready cash or an unlimited credit card like her girlfriends, Rodrigo suggests.

Rodrigo is well positioned to have a credible view on this subject, since he doesn't have access to his father's money, his father being not only a thief but also a homophobe. For example, Rodrigo is forbidden from hanging out in their famous hôtel particulier without the rest of the family being there, unlike his brothers, who are always free to invite their little girlfriends for weekends in Paris. Ever since he was a kid, Rodrigo has had to deal with the frequent verbal abuse ridiculing all his mannerisms, which reveal his sweet, almost shy personality. This has made him a better person, not a worse one. Suffering does have a transformative power, but that power is neutral, it can go any which way, and often that direction's random, repressed someplace in the unconscious, and before we know it, there we are. Ana Cândida is stagnated, her attempt at change occurs only on the surface, motivated by some external demands, it's not an existential concern. She has so little self-awareness, I don't think she even knows she's fat.

The other day, at a party, she sat down next to me and launched into a preprepared speech, which she must have thought my friends and I would like: You know, Vivian, the Brazilian elite is so ignorant, they just don't value culture at all, total nightmare. These people dream of living in Miami. It used to be much better before—people collected art, they had books in the house, everyone wanted to be European, not American . . . As I listened to her, all I could think about was how much I was going to have to spend on Botox, seeing how my facial expression contorted with every line she spoke. My dermatologist had advised me to ease up on my smiling to avoid wrinkles, so can you imagine if she'd seen me like that, practically a Shar-Pei? At my last appointment, I told her I couldn't do it, I'm a terrible actress, easier just to keep my distance, once again, from Ana Cândida.

4

When I was a little girl, I was always good, I did everything right, I never made any terrible faux pas, like using an Aladdin backpack when it was the year of Pocahontas. School supplies tracked the calendar of the year's movies exactly. It was like a kids' version of fashion week. From the age of ten, the codes move a few steps closer to the adult world, becoming every bit as rigid as any dinner placement, the themed backpacks replaced by T-shirts that announced their prices in the logos printed in big letters: CALVIN KLEIN, DONNA KARAN, RALPH LAUREN. I obeyed it all, my acceptance should have been guaranteed. So why was I suddenly unable to communicate with my friends? Something was shifting from that model, which, till then, had seemed so Cartesian, action and reaction, act and consequence, like a language in which I broadcast some sounds and the other person immediately understands. Out of nowhere, everything I said sounded weird, like it was from another universe or it was just plain ridiculous. The sudden switch from happy child to melancholy adolescent seemed too absolute to be just your usual expression of puberty. I went to see a doctor, after that a psychologist, and then a psychiatrist, and every diagnosis was the same: a mental illness. The solution was simple—a little medication, that's all, no different from an aspirin, and in a few months, a year at most, I'd go back to being a normal girl. Except that wasn't what happened; on the contrary, I got worse. So this depression that was getting consolidated more and more intensely, was it rooted in something social, chemical, or existential?

Marina Falcão says I've always been too pathologized. Maybe my parents had gotten traumatized by having to pause our lives for a year to treat my toxoplasmosis when I was nine months old. I had another problem when I was still a baby, too, something in my intestine, and needed a biopsy. Every pregnant woman looks at her belly and gives that same hopeful sigh: this baby's gonna be perfect. But what's born is an imperfect human, with its own desires, disobedient, rebellious, like a doll that arrives already broken, and you can't send it back. The toxoplasmosis returned a decade later, attacking my eyeball. The vision in my right eye went almost completely. And then came the crying fits, the sudden shyness, verging on mutism, the fear of going to school, the struggle to keep up with my subjects. Obviously the phenomena are interconnected, but I don't really remember. The depression could be a result of the cortisone from the treatment, which would be a logical, chemical, objective explanation. It's comfortable and categorizable: nobody's fault, we did everything right, we just lost out in the lottery, our daughter is sick. I wish my memories of that time weren't so sparse so I could articulate a coherent narrative. I don't know if it's right to call it trauma—I've always accepted everything so stoically, so obedient to my prescriptions, twenty pills a day, with lunch and dinner. And not long after that came the distress at the realization that my personality was not forming as expected.

Along with the medication, Maria Elisa resorted to a whole load of different things to improve my social skills: theater class, dance class, painting class, gymnastics class, meditation, sing therapy, yoga, Reiki. There were other activities, too, which were more, let's say, mystical, like paying visits to cloistered nuns, exorcism sessions, trips to the sanctuaries of Fátima, Lourdes, Aparecida. Above all, I was categorically forbidden from revealing to other people that I was seeing a psychiatrist. But it was no use, people could tell. During recess, I had crying fits in the bathroom stall—I'd spend that half hour sitting on the toilet, staring straight at the door forty centimeters from my face, or squatting on the dirty floor, under the toilet paper dispenser, staring at my own vomit caused by the side effects of all the meds. What was left of the Ruffles floating in a dull, dirty liquid. This was every day until the bell rang, and I'd stick a piece of gum in my mouth to take away the bad stomach breath, pinch my cheeks back to a healthy pink, and return to math class. Marina Falcão, running out of patience, interrupts my account: Vivian, you have depression, not anemia. And you were crying and throwing up, so you were red already. Oh man, but it's so clear, the memory of me looking at myself in the mirror over the sink, hoping to find some trick to hide what had just happened. Should I maybe wash my face with cold water to get rid of the puffiness? It's hard to define precisely, if no one saw it, then nothing happened, I'd keep telling myself. And just like that, a whole life is lived under the rug. If the people around me didn't see my daily crying, like actually see it with their own eyes, and they didn't receive the explicit information that I had some mental illness, it was like none of it existed.

Often enough, some doctor would say it was just my low threshold for frustration. My mother alternated between believing that verdict and blaming me for my inability to keep up with my schoolwork. Now we need you to stop being spoiled, she'd say, and she'd give the whole big speech that was completely focused on the chemistry of the brain, then she'd go running to the doctor whenever my behavior got slightly out of control again, asking to increase the meds. Maria Elisa would wonder: How can Vivian be depressed if I can hear her laughing out loud when she's locked in her room watching *Friends*? And the psychiatrist would start up again with bipolar, cyclothymia, even border-line personality disorder, and once again everything was going to be okay, because now there was something new to be identified. Who knows what my personality would be like if I wasn't so medicated, 'cause I don't have a lot of memories from before the toxoplasmosis. It's like the time before was this past life I could only access via a vague intuition that was not very reliable, that could easily be invaded by fiction.

I was a twelve-year-old baby, imipramine hydro-chloride gave birth to me, and each time the medication got changed I would reincarnate in the same body, with alterations in behavior that were outside my control. And like this, my parents could create a new version of me, just one pill away, until they'd gotten rid of all the sadness, the disgust, the distress, the hunger, the judg-ments of the neighbors, of the fellow members of the golf club and the Búzios set. The ideal Vivian Noronha would be thin, but without the binge eating caused by the latest antipsychotic, sociable to the correct de-gree, always smiling, none of the alarming fits of rage

from that goddamn venlafaxine, top of her class, thank
you, Ritalin. The Topamax didn't really work out—it
increased my suicidal thoughts, more or less curbed my
appetite, I was suddenly eating one mozzarella di bu-
fala per day, no more, the perfect counterpoint to the
Zyprexa. My parents believed I'd be happier if I was
compliant, and was therefore accepted. Those medication changes were really hard on me. The old Vivian
was constantly getting buried by traits that would catch
me by surprise. Maria Elisa kept up the hope that, despite all the setbacks, we'd find the perfect combination
that would transform me into the ideal baby she had
never conceived.

There are certain details that take on such excessive proportions that they disrupt the familial peace.
Maria Elisa would cling to small frictions of a practical
nature, like the fact of my being right-handed when it
came to writing, but left-handed when it came to eating.
At every meal she'd say it again: Honestly, it makes
no sense, you must try to be aware of unconscious
patterns. I'm going to sign you up at once for Neuro-
linguistic Programming. Your grandmother, for all
her flaws, was a very wise woman and she always said
you don't change temperament, you change behavior.
Quite so! Still not content with this, Mom would go
on, at any moment in the day, imposing her diktats:
You need to be racée, don't use such high heels, don't

wear such short dresses, don't paint your nails red, oh,
it's just horrendous, so vulgar. Vivian, you really must
make eye contact, you're always so still, silent, distant,
it's almost like you're autistic. Shyness is only accept-
able up to the age of six, after that it's just a lack of prac-
tice. I'm going to put you into a modeling course just
so you stop dragging yourself around like a rhinoceros.
Don't walk like a cowboy, don't greet people like such
a brute, don't talk about your own life. The main trick
of seduction is to ask about the other person's inter-
ests, mind you, never forget that. Don't go out without
combing your hair. You should always be soignée, it's
a sign of respect to others. Don't keep saying in public
that you don't want to have children, it's most unpleas-
ant. No man's going to want you like that. Don't do gay
activism online, people might mistake you for a lesbian,
and then how will you manage? I mean, I'm not ho-
mophobic, I mean sometimes, okay, but not a lot. Right
then, that's it, you start CBT next week.

At twelve, not long after I was diagnosed with depression and started taking mood stabilizers, I picked
up a habit that I personally still think is inoffensive
but really bothered my parents. At night, when everyone else was ready for bed, I'd stay in the living room
by myself, reading a book, and when some idea caught
my attention, I'd walk around the dining table to di-
gest my thoughts, then I'd go to the study, where our

lovely English library had a view of the sea, and then
loop back. If the idea was stimulating enough, I'd speed
up, sometimes even run, do these little jumps, press my
heels against the parquet floor, and in my euphoria, I'd
often crash into the wall, using my hands to absorb
the impact, which would leave a subtle mark on the
paintwork, then I'd turn around and open the fridge.
Everybody opens the fridge to think. Everybody does
little jumps when they're running spontaneously. But
for some reason, my modus operandi caused huge
consternation in the family, to the point where it led
to meetings on the subject with a view to some inter-
vention. What are the neighbors going to think, that
we've got a horse in the apartment? Dad would ask, or
Mom, or Grandma. Honestly, what does it matter what
the neighbors think? It's not like they're our friends,
the noise is only in the living room, it's several yards
from the bedrooms, it doesn't disturb anybody's sleep.
And besides, it's a way of relieving anxiety that doesn't
cost anything, wouldn't it be worse if I took it out on
clothes, booze, drugs, sex, even teen pregnancy? But
this nonstop walking around the dining table was un-
heard of, a thing that didn't happen in movies, on TV,
in commercials. It was brought both to family therapy
and to my psychiatrist: Vivian's got to take another
medication to stop her walking like that and doing

those little jumps, Maria Elisa would say. And I'd push back, because I *liked* walking like that, it did me good, why take extra medication, with possible side effects, just 'cause the neighbors might find it weird?

Within the family unit, expulsion was inconceivable, because the love between parents and children is natural, unconditional, compulsory. I don't know whether the obligatory love between family members is worth as much as genuine love, but what is that real love, anyway? No one ever knows. It's paradoxical, an abstract feeling, which is limitless, as my mother likes saying when smothering me with kisses, but it's also confined within a structure that's rigid, necessarily limited. We try to emulate an idea of love, but we're in the dark, all we're left with is this intense feeling, which can sometimes be pleasurable—and we also gain a kind of moral sheen, as a bonus. Even when I was a teenager, and already adult-sized, my mother would hug me against my will—she'd squeeze me tight, like I was a teddy bear, inanimate. It was pointless saying no, no, no, it was a gesture of affection, how lucky I was, my mom really loves me. Any attempt to extricate myself by force would've been considered aggressive. And at a suitable moment, a moment of calm and physical distance, maybe when we were separated by a formal table in a stylish restaurant, if I happened to mention how

suffocating I found it, both literally and metaphor-
ically, I'd be considered cold and insensitive, even
wicked.

It's the rule of the game: if you refuse to take part
in the narrative, well, you'd better be prepared. There's
not going to be any explicit rejection, but rather a limbo,
a vacuum, a strange mix of love, or at least what we understand as love, but also anger, confusion, and resent-
ment. They keep repeating it, automatically: You're our
daughter, we love you, we accept you, we want you to be
happy. And they do think it's true, they just don't know
how to act, how to think. Seems the baby has refused to
sign the contract granting the family reparation for all
the time and money spent on that small human being.
Every one of us is in the mergers and acquisitions business. Before falling asleep, when dreams mingle with
conscious thoughts, memories of the day that's just
happened and plans for tomorrow, my father or mother
must think, about me: Oh, Vivian, darling, you're so
nuts, but so loved, you're responsible for decades of investment gone down the drain. And if they're cynical,
or have a sense of humor, they'd conclude: Maybe we
should've just bought a boat.

5

On Sundays, our family used to go to a church that was
some way from home, where the Mass was short, never
more than forty minutes, and there was parking right
there in the courtyard. At the Paz de Cristo we'd greet
smiling acquaintances and friends in the front pews like
it was a little party, a bit of social joy. Only the Com-
munion was more solemn, demanding an ambiguous
posture, humble on the one hand, as represented by the
slow steps, lowered heads, contained gestures, a discreet
procession on the perfect red carpet, but it also required
clothes, hair, skin that were impeccable, always, and
not necessarily out of respect for Jesus. It's funny, the
priest seemed like kind of a commie—whenever he got
the chance, he'd drop these insinuations against all those
pharisees. Made no difference, obviously, since no one
was listening, they were concerned with other things.
Even in the pulpit, with the spotlight, the outfit, and

the authority, with the whole mise-en-scène calibrated to intimidate the audience, he was still just an accessory to those people, an extra no more important than a waiter, whose interaction is limited to the serving of wine, at most. On the way out, the chat between friends and acquaintances could stretch on for nearly an hour, and who knows, maybe just go right on into dinner, an informal Sunday pizza. I know that some of those people were important for my father's professional life, hence the need to be present, independent of anything the homily might contain. Most significantly, this was the Mass attended by the family of Mimi de la Blétière.

According to one society columnist, Mimi de la Blétière talks with equal devotion about God and about Ibrahim Sued. It was all but impossible not to make fun of the ample repertoire of expressions that Mimi coined. Modesty apart, the sky was so gorgeous this morning, not a cloud! she used to say. It was really a Freudian slip: Mimi was a kind of informal customs officer to that social microcosm. Her power of veto and approval were practically godlike among her peers. The weekly meeting to pray the rosary at her house was a compulsory initiation ritual for anyone who wanted to be a part of that milieu. Her "signature look" made her stand out from the other socialites: loose clothing, always in pastel colors, flowing scarves, sky-blue eye shadow that covered the whole surface of her eyelids to match her irises, and some mighty jewels, not at all inconspicuous. According to my friend Rodrigo, Mimi de la Blétière was doing Our Lady of Grace cosplay.

Her life philosophy: God created the little pink impatiens and He created the imperial palms. That was the mantra she kept repeating to her seven children. This determinism was absolutely rigid for sociopolitical matters, yet somehow didn't seem to apply to her own personal life. It was like the small claims court worked particularly effectively in matters of divine justice. For example, Mimi was always bothered by her narrow yard, which didn't have space for a swimming pool. And then you had that next-door plot, which was so huge, and occupied only by this one little cottage, so very tiny, frightfully délabrée! Wagner Pereira, her husband, was just a generic rich man, with a talent for business but kind of muted, with no great personality; he's real honorable, though, he's a genuine person, authentic, who doesn't hide his origins, he's always telling stories from his childhood. Wagner Pereira surfed on his wife's natural charisma, and echoed her claims: At this rate, I wouldn't be surprised if this guy started to bring property values down around here. Mimi, then, decided to take action. She made the neighbor a proposal, one that was somewhat generous, but which was promptly refused. Mimi prayed, and prayed, and prayed. The neighbor was run over and killed the following month. Since his children were arguing over the inheritance, they reached a deal for half the price originally proposed, on condition the purchase be concluded at once, in cash. If You Just Believe. Mimi's swimming pool got built. God sees all.

It was a major family triumph when my sister, Laura, married Eudes de la Blétière. They both had physical features reminiscent of childhood: him with the silky blond hair, side-parted, impeccable, and those prominent rosy cheeks, which made him look fat despite being thin; her with the angular face, petite build, an almost preadolescent body, faintly anorexic, looking short despite being tall. A couple who gave the impression of being kind of sexless. The romance started up when they were traveling with a gang of friends to the Hamptons. Laura had done her master's at Princeton, worked at Monsanto in St. Louis, then got hired by Bayer and went back to New York (she was living on the Upper West Side). Eudes was an employee at Goldman Sachs. Originally they planned to form a power couple, a proposal that was actually kind of subversive, given that young women in that group followed one of three paths: a decorative profession, demanding few hours of work, like jewelry designer, poet, or image consultant; or a career that could even be successful, but only in strictly feminine areas like fashion or cake-making; or some other profession, so long as it got abandoned the moment the first kids showed up.

They lost control of that narrative in 2012 when they returned to Brazil and Laura got elevated to the directorship of the Samarco mining company, while Eudes settled into some midlevel role at Santander. From then on, they developed a plan whereby it wouldn't be clear that the couple's alpha/beta dynamic was reversed: it was she who paid for the apartment, bilingual school for the kids, the maid, their driver, travel—in short, the bulk of their expenses—while he produced his credit card when they were dining out with friends. Later, when he got canned and spent almost a year unemployed, the performance continued unchanged, but the credit card that he used, in reality, belonged to Laura. Often enough, people outside their original circle believed that my sister had married a very rich man who bankrolled her extravagances. The couple didn't deny this; on the contrary, they even subtly encouraged it. In this version, Laura wasn't the slightly plain wife of a poor schmuck who lived off her parents' allowance, but a lucky woman who'd won the love of a prince. Laura, in the eyes of the world, must have had some je ne sais quoi about her—I mean, can you even imagine, hooking such a great catch, with breeding and means! It was almost like she was some Wallis Simpson type, pampered by her rich husband: bags, shoes, trips, works of art. And thus had she attained the ultimate status symbols of classic femininity.

At eighteen, Laura spent a few months working as a sales assistant at Daslu in São Paulo. It was a rite of passage for all the girls of that generation, at least before the scandals, tax evasion, federal police, etc. For this, it was worth moving to São Paulo, drawing on any useful contacts, deferring her studies at PUC till the second semester. During this period, she was living with our plump aunt, one of the store's biggest customers, and I'm sure that helped her get the job. Laura spent her whole salary before she'd even left the building. Having a Chanel 2.55 was quite essential. Mom used to say: There's nothing more middle class than tossing away all your meager savings on that sort of thing, it's a sign of insecurity. My mom has a better understanding of class dynamics than many people in my dad's family. She can go around acting like she's the heiress to a great fortune who just doesn't want to flaunt her money, when in reality, she never had all that much to begin with. Her parents, who have already died, were university professors—and Marxists, according to her! Which, now that I think about it, does make some sense.

Laura started interning at a family friend's stockbrokers in her very first term of university. Her commitment to success was propelled by a discipline that was so stoic. She didn't drink, she didn't smoke, didn't use drugs, didn't eat meat, she did yoga and Pilates, played tennis and squash. Every month she'd wander in with

a new bag or pair of shoes. She never spent any time at
our family's modest beach house because some invita-
tion always showed up to travel to Angra with somebody or other who owned an island there. Vicky, her
best friend, lived in a house that took up a whole block
in Leblon, though she used to never pay the candy seller
who had a little stall outside their school—this totally
adorable, toothless little man. The girl used to say she
didn't have any cash on her, always with this big smile
on her face, that total self-confidence of someone who's
never been rejected, and a convincing affectation that
mixed persuasion with theater, like she was practicing
to take on her daddy's firm. And then she'd forget all
about it. Laura felt sorry, she'd pay her friend's debts,
sometimes she'd buy an extra ice cream to help the guy
out, ask him about his life. Her empathy didn't trans-
late into annoyance and she never expressed any kind
of criticism; it didn't stop her from being at Vicky's side
every weekend, motorboat rides, horseback riding on
the farm, skiing at Aspen. At most, when she was at
home, she'd make a little patronizing comment: Oh,
poor Vicky, she's so out of touch, it probably doesn't
even occur to her that the dear little man needs that
change for his bus fare. Then she would immediately
romanticize the man's hardship: Such dignity!

Intuitively, Laura was implementing a concept
that's easy to find around the world's main metropoles:

keeping a rich person in tow. It's common among middle-class people—upper-middle-class people, that is, people who are also kind of rich but not *properly* rich. After all, let's not kid ourselves, one does need some minimum budget to sustain certain extravagances. A rich person kept in tow will lend out their helicopter, put you up in their Paris apartment, invite you for a Corsican boat trip. In exchange, a simple mortal's got to be constantly cheerful, never complaining, up for anything, like some children's party entertainer who lives to please their rich person. And the power relationship is circular, 'cause the rich are incredibly needy. In a way, Vicky needs Laura more than Laura does Vicky. Sometimes, the shot backfires, when, out of nowhere, they suddenly decide to split the restaurant check fifty-fifty, so it's a thousand euro a head, no matter who ordered the salad and who the truffles, who drank wine and who water, who is a banking heir and who lives on their salary. Vicky's kind of perverse, she enjoyed doing that sort of thing to Laura. But if you did all the math, adding up all the variables, even the hard-to-measure ones, it was still totally worth it.

Laura turned out to be an excellent investment, she proved profitable. The whole thing had been money well spent: the extra-special trousseau, the ballet classes, the wedding party at the golf club, five hundred guests in the main hall, a number considered modest and in-

timate, only close friends, only the right people. Her
role as daughter is carried out expertly—she plays the
part she's been assigned very well, that contract signed
in her name when she was registered as a Noronha. But
how can you expect a baby who can't read or write to
be aware of all these clauses? Committing to such arbitrary rules is no joke. A whole existence just to please
a group of people who they themselves consider shal-
low, foolish, inelegant. Money attracts contacts who
attract money, which buys the pictures that decorate
the house, which impresses guests, for the whole cy-
cle to start up again, like this kind of pyramid scheme
where different types of capital get accumulated, each
helping the other, like they're climbing a flight of stairs
hand in hand, so adorable and cooperative, and we go
on, with the promise that one day, maybe one day, the
money can be spent not on an investment or moments
of superficial pleasure that just atrophy our existence,
the smallness of always always always expecting something in exchange from the universe, but instead on
some carefree enjoyment, with no interest in results,
just whatever swells the soul, transcending the petty
preoccupations of sociability, honestly anything at all.
And look, I'm only advocating for a new way of spending money, it's not exactly revolutionary. But for that,
we're going to need other learnings that are not available to us right now.

6

Sex was always a no-go subject in my house. For a long time, even as a kid, my mom used to come into my bedroom unexpectedly, to check on my hands. If they weren't in view, she'd lift the blanket, abruptly, almost aggressive. Often enough, I was in fact masturbating, even if I didn't know what that meant, and it was just feelings. Over the years, as childhood got left further behind and I was exposed to unfiltered images from the adult world, those feelings would be accompanied by fantasies, many of them forbidden, which I didn't even admit to my analyst, scared of some unwanted revelation; what if those fantasies were symptoms of some abnormality and I'd need to take even more medication, some combo of antidepressants to pacify my desires, making them legible and tame? Or alternatively, even worse, what if I was forced to undergo some treatments that were painful, embarrassing, humiliating? It was only much later I learned that those sexual fantasies didn't make me into some kind of Marquis de Sade. On the contrary, they were perfectly common, almost normative, clichéd.

At that more vulnerable age, every inappropriate touch, every lustful picture that popped into my mind, always treacherously and inadvertently, was accompanied by a sudden invasion of terror and guilt. I'd beg forgiveness, make little deals, twenty minutes of sexual thoughts and in exchange I'd pray the rosary, and if it was some especially sinful perversion, I'd do all three parts. On my bedside table, I had this improvised nativity scene with assorted extra angels and saints that my mom would bring back from her trips, each in a different material and style, and one time I even tried putting them away in the cupboard so I wouldn't have to face my own sin, but the next day, there they were again, ready to judge me. Whenever I heard the noise of the door handle, followed by the creaking of the old hinges, I'd quickly whip my arms out, positioning them parallel to my body, rigid as a corpse or prostrate, and still Maria Elisa would question me: What were you doing? she would ask sharply, her voice wavering, like she didn't know how to act either: Your hand is a little stinky. Even her scolding infantilized me.

At twenty-two, I lost my virginity to a guy I'd met at Vicky's wedding party. He was very cute, a cousin of the bride's, and even though he was my age, he was there as best man, alongside my sister, who was single at the time, as maid-of-honor. He said: My folks just gave me an apartment, in São Conrado. It's got two bedrooms, a real nice veranda, cool view of the mountain. Come with me, we can light one up, have a nice quiet chat. I've got my car, I can drop you back after, safe and sound. I was so dumb, I didn't even get that the whole thing was a euphemism for sex. The act itself was an uncomfortable, bureaucratic kind of experience. I felt indifferent about it. Then, instead of taking me home as he'd promised, he rolled over and fell asleep. That wasn't what we'd agreed. What do you think I am, I asked, some kind of prostitute? My moralism was genuine, I really was that woman. Seriously, girl, how old *are* you?! I thought you were an adult, but apparently I was wrong, he muttered, before shutting the bedroom door in my face and leaving me alone in the living room.

At eleven thirty the next morning I went down to the entrance hall and wandered the condo's internal road, beside the well-tended lawn, by the children's playground and the communal swimming pool, kind of lost amid that succession of identical buildings. When I reached the guardhouse, unsure how to get out, I just stood in front of the fast lane, unable to cross the road, nowhere to turn a corner. Above the gate, a convex mirror was distorting my tragic, seedy, disgusting image: the sequined silk dress, my legs without nylons, hair disheveled, eyes smudged with mascara, my lipstick smeared. I was right, he wasn't: it was the perfect depiction of a prostitute in a movie.

I was never going to get a boyfriend, not after that. I did want to get a boyfriend, and then marry, get out of the house, maybe go live abroad, on another continent, far from the rest of the family, I'd finally be rid of all that oppressiveness, could I maybe marry a diplomat? Not anymore, not unless someone totally unaware showed up, someone well-mannered but without any mutual friends, unfamiliar with my history. I'd have to find another road, go someplace my reputation didn't matter, 'cause I was never going to be able to go back home, and now I didn't have school anymore, I wouldn't be welcome anymore, I'd need to find another family, but how, now that I was never going to be able to get myself a boyfriend? Forty minutes later, a cab came past.

Back home, I found the same mother who used to police my masturbation. Fifteen years on, she was still the same person, or even worse, as I was now the realization of her worst fears, the rude, slutty daughter, the reminder that she should have been stricter, the proof of her failure. The whole city's looking for you. I called all your friends. Don't you dare lie to me, Vivian: Did a boy see you naked? In tears, I answered yes, and told her about the unkept promise to give me a ride back home. I thought my mom was going to call me a tramp, and maybe she did. But in my memory, the most explosive thing was her rage at the guy, that little swine, the swine, the swine! It was like a mother's reaction to her daughter getting raped. I mean, according to her always odd choice of words, getting raped by a boy. My state of confusion at how she dealt with it lasted days. If I'd had the maturity, I could have retorted: Chill, Mom, he's just some jerk, just like all the others, and anyway the sex was good, it was only the post-coitus that wasn't.

After that day, my mom took me for my first visit to her longtime gynecologist. Not even at my first menstruation had the subject come up. We went together, I did the tests, everything worked out fine, and I left with a prescription for an anti-HPV vaccine. A thousand reais for a vaccine?! Let's wait till next month, it won't make any difference, said my mom, like it was impossible I might screw somebody over the course of those days. For a while, I tried to hold her to it, and either the subject was aborted or she pretended to be busy. It was a bit much spending all that money just to deal with her own daughter cluelessly screwing her way around the city. Maybe, if the idea went out of her head, her daughter would remain immaculate, and there'd be no reason to worry about catching anything. And the thousand reais could go toward a pair of shoes.

For many years, I avoided sharing that story, especially with my friends, who were girls, and straight, with emotional trajectories I envied, because they'd lost their virginities to their boyfriends while they were still teenagers. I imagined they'd discovered sexuality with somebody they loved and trusted, naturally. To be honest, I tried not to even think about this story, and when, unintentionally, it resurfaced, a picture would form in my head of myself lying there, motionless and scared, staring up at the ceiling, the naked man penetrating me, and a supercut of all the times I had sex in a similar way, like a mummy, or like a woman who's getting raped, even if that obviously wasn't the case. Before the penetration, when the faceless boy went down on me, I felt the greatest pleasure of my life, and I don't think anything will ever match that feeling again. Today, the only time I need to fake an orgasm is when someone's going down on me.

7

Alberto Barbosa Ribas was the godfather who baptized me. Often enough, when Dad was in some financial trouble, running the risk that he might need to sell a painting, a small retail unit downtown, or, even worse, a house, it was Uncle Alberto who came to his rescue. His job is buying companies that are about to go under, and Uncle Alberto has so many companies that he can always find Dad a spot on the management or the board. My family refers to this with some detachment, like it's a kind of hobby, like collecting stamps or old maps, vinyl records, shipyards, cold storage, or oil companies. When Dad is touched at the friendship between them, I'm almost sure it's because a substantial amount of our money exists only because of Uncle Alberto. The trajectories of money are always slightly shady, like in alchemy. What's left is the matter, the result, the visible, it is the word that is made flesh and lives among us.

Recently, it was a publisher of women's magazines, who had let a dozen employees go, with their wages delayed and severance they'll never receive. The elevator operator, who had cancer, was forced to stop his treatment because of the sudden absence of a health-care plan. The story went viral, the internet was moved, some donations came in, and finally they managed to get at least enough money for the radiotherapy. Maria Elisa was so dreadfully concerned that she even made a generous contribution herself, and when she learned of the positive outcome, she was pleased, relieved, and lit a candle, she said everything in life works itself out, thank God.

At sixteen, I went to the birthday party of Vicky's younger sister, in Búzios. I wasn't invited, exactly. I was in the city over the holidays, three days with my parents already. That Saturday, Maria Elisa informed me that I'd been invited, which was weird, I didn't know anyone, only enough to say "Hey, how's it going?" at the most. It was probably a favor between adults that had little to do with me. They didn't tell us the timing, or the plans, we assumed it'd be a dinner or something, and when I arrived, at seven, the "late luncheon" had already finished. Only the torta alemã was left for dessert. Later, when the adults had gone to sleep, we went to the TV room to play cards, video games, charades. There were eight of us girls and three boys, Uncle

Alberto's son Albertinho among them. At one point, somebody brought a bottle of vodka from the kitchen and suggested we play Truth or Consequences. After a bit of reluctance, everyone agreed.

In this version of the game, a little different from the traditional version, you could refuse to answer, but as a consequence, you had to take a drink. It seemed Albertinho had some privileged information about my life, 'cause all his questions were real specific. Years before, during my early adolescence, Uncle Alberto had needed to intercede to enable my countless changes of school, almost always in the middle of the academic year, as an emergency measure. To begin with, Albertinho just asked, with no apparent malice: Say, how come you changed schools in April, not in the normal month? I was evasive: I'd gotten sick. Then he went further, wanted to know what illness, and I kept quiet, preferring to drink. Then, when it was the others' turn, I calmed down, and the subjects related to other things, gossip, friendships, pot, kissing, sex. But soon Albertinho was back in charge: Are you autistic? and I answered no, and in the next round: Do you have some kind of mental illness? And so as not to expose myself, just like Mom taught me, I drank the vodka. The interrogation got more and more inappropriate, embarrassing, perverse, a mix of correct hunches and wrong ones, like he had only part of the information and didn't just want to discover the rest but also reveal it to his audience. Do you take psychiatric medicine? Have you ever been in a mental hospital? Have you attempted suicide? Have you ever cut your own arm with a knife? At the time, I thought the answers were yes, even if in reality they were no, but just to be on the safe side, to preserve my privacy, I drank the vodka, three glasses in a row and I don't know how many before that, and on an empty stomach.

I was always a hopeless suicide. At the most, wishing to escape from the oppression that is an entire bedroom lined in pink toile de Jouy, I'd sit on the windowsill, with the building's courtyard twenty meters below me, smoking cigarettes without inhaling, trying for some kind of glamour. On top of the air conditioner, which was hanging outside the window, sat an ashtray where I'd stub out the almost intact cigarettes, it was like I had my own nice little bedside table just for me, suspended in the air. At other times, in more daring moments, I'd yank the laces out of my sneakers and improvise a gallows somewhere, the top cupboard, the plaster chandelier, wherever. With the rope around my neck, up on my tiptoes, I'd try to knock over the swivel chair, and it would slide around, producing a blast of adrenaline like it was some kind of extreme sport, like parachuting. If anything did happen, I'd need only shout and my mom would hear.

And in fact, one day, she did hear, and it was horrible, a family meeting was assembled, the psychiatrist called in on emergency even though it was a Sunday. In the bathroom, I cried in front of the mirror, compulsive and silent, analyzing my deformed red face, which was almost beautiful in its foulness, like a long-suffering engraving by Goya. As punishment, or that's how it seemed to me at the time, I got interned in a psychiatric clinic on the edge of the city. First thing I thought when I saw my room was that this must be what prisons are like in Norway. Eight square meters, a neatly made single bed, a comfortable quilt, a table and a chair for reading. The window was barred despite being only on the second floor. Nobody was going to kill themselves jumping from that height, at most they'd break their foot, making it impossible to run away, the sole purpose of the grille was humiliation, to remind you this wasn't a hospital, let alone a hotel, not even one of those super simple, basic ones you get near the airport, but a clinic for people who are mentally ill.

The first moments in the clinic were all about the boredom. For you to think about your attitude, not to repeat this nonsense, never, ever again. I don't suppose you want to be stigmatized as problematic forever, Mom said, sitting on the chair close to the bed, with the clinic psychologist standing beside her. The next afternoon, following an unsuccessful nap, I walked across the hallway and into the common room, which was lit up in a cold white light. There was a ping-pong table, but nobody was playing ping-pong, they were just resignedly watching Faustão's regular Sunday show on the TV. I somehow managed to get permission to call home from the phone in the stairwell. I screamed, desperate, that I wasn't crazy, I swear I'm normal, I swear I'll try to be normal, I swear I'll never try to kill myself ever again for the rest of my life.

The pressure to conceal this history of mine was so great it was like I'd committed a murder. I needed to preserve my reputation, better to drink the vodka and retain my right to remain silent. I don't know how long it was before I found myself in the hallway throwing up while somebody tried to get me to the bathroom. The rest of the night I don't remember at all apart from odd flashes. No idea how long I spent unconscious, maybe an hour or two, or twenty minutes. In the cab, heading home, a couple of girls were saying something about the night: And Albertinho, he was so irresponsible, kind of an actual scumbag? Vivian literally could've died, can you imagine! And when they said my name, I remembered him offering me a glass of water while I was throwing up: It tastes like vodka, but it's water. You can drink it, trust me, it'll do you good. And so I chugged a tall glass of pure vodka before passing out. At the time, Mom played down the situation, saying, oh, it was just one of those teenager things, and insisting I shouldn't cause problems: He's just a mean little boy, you guys don't need to be close, you don't even need to be friendly with him, just be polite, nice, say hello, smile. I really don't want to risk a quarrel between your father and Uncle Alberto.

By 2014 everybody involved in that episode had grown up, they were full-grown adults, with jobs in a bank, a lawyer's office, an advertising agency, some of them married, with kids on the way. And that is when Albertinho reappeared in my life, or rather, on my Facebook page. One morning, when I woke up, I noticed that my simple post on the presidential election had transformed into a heated discussion, like a hundred comments, with the nightlife queers, the conceptual artists, the theater folk, and the private bankers and equity managers all jumbled together. While Albertinho was ranting about corruption, Alex was receiving a file with the irregular activities carried out by the families of each individual who was participating in the opposite end of the argument, all of it documented in trustworthy newspapers and magazines, citing the relevant legal proceedings. When at last he posted each piece of news, he concluded with a comment aimed at Albertinho & co.: *I am hopeful we can keep this group you represent and that you make up (market-fundamentalist, selfish, greedy, anti-poor, segregationist, racist, status-obsessed, delusional, and ignorant) as far from federal power as possible. As far as is *actually* possible, that is, 'cause we* *all know how hard it is to attain any social achievement without greasing the palms of those in power. So I hope you people will stay in your lanes (financial market, gym, fashion blog, marbled shopping malls, private booth in some tacky nightclub, etc.) and earn yourselves a load of money and not make the whole country mad by talking shit 'cause we need to move forward and, man, you guys are having a *serious* meltdown right now.*

In retaliation, Albertinho posted photos on his page of that distant night, which show me throwing up, my blouse askew, part of my breast visible, the fly of my jeans open, panties showing, hair disheveled, my face pale, practically blue, right before I passed out. When Maria Elisa heard about this, she got worried and was more affectionate than the previous time—after all, she could no longer play the mean little boy card, but still her verdict was: Forget about it.

In my mother's head, taking care of my well-being always involved giving me trips, five-star hotels, expensive restaurants, top-quality clothes, and all this depended on Uncle Alberto. It never occurred to her or Dad that they were prioritizing one relationship to the detriment of another. I'm not even sure whether at times like those I would have wanted them to take a position defending my honor, I mean, I know it sounds kind of ridiculous. But at the very least a half defense, even just a timid one, something merely symbolic, an act behind closed doors would have been enough, just among the family, for me to believe, at least for five minutes, that I am more important than us staying at the Plaza Athénée.

A whole existence trying to please a group of people who are unable to produce any affection that isn't run through with money and power. This requires taking part in certain specific rituals, which make up a strict choreography played out in a circular way: money becomes access, which becomes more money. And one day, you never know, at some highly coveted dinner at the home of one of those customs-women who controls access into and out of that microcosm, you are rewarded with the best seat at the table, next to the hostess. It seems dumb, and it is, but it's a reason for living, a purpose for life, and like some perpetual game, with the dinner placements as stages for progressing on the board, there are hands dealt that are worth points, some more, others less, there are victories and defeats, and it's exciting. Superficial people experience great suffering, too, their pain is profound, it tears their souls apart. Dad must spend so many hours deep in the distress of wondering why he wasn't invited to Vicky's husband's fiftieth birthday party. He's number two in his father-in-law's steel company, it's important that he's there. Could it be I'm not rich enough, important enough, maybe I'm too close to some rival of his, maybe I didn't fawn over the guy, I was too subtle in that endeavor, almost polite, I shouldn't have allowed my honor to get the upper hand, and now this, it's practically a social murder. And then, in the tiniest fraction of a second, his whole life flashes before his eyes. That, they say, is what happens when you die.

8

On my birthday, Laura threw me a surprise party at her apartment, which had been recently renovated by a trendy architect, and was full of works of art. All the guests were people in top jobs in galleries and museums: some of them genuinely close to me, others barely acquaintances, whom I'd never spoken to for even five minutes.

Some I'd have liked to have gotten to know better, as they did have an aura about them, with interesting trajectories, stories to tell. There was this one lady, a set designer, raised in an artistic milieu, goddaughter to a French movie director, married five times, always to notable figures. Apparently delighted to be talking about it all, too. Before I was born, she was saying, my parents went to a party and Ingrid Bergman was there, she put her hand on my mom's belly, she asked the baby's name, and I was baptized right there and then, in tribute to

her. My sister was listening, rapt, marveling, asking questions, spinning compliments, even though
the whole thing wasn't giving us any great reflections
and was basically just a roll call of names: When I was
twenty, I met my first husband, he was my dad's age,
and I decided to get pregnant right away, because I
knew that, being an alcoholic the way he was, the man
wouldn't last long, and I wanted to ensure the continu-
ity of a line of geniuses.

Marina Falcão always says anybody who likes to
hang out with people who are considered interesting
isn't interesting, what they are is self-interested. As if
they think great qualities are transferred by osmosis.
No such thing as meritocracy, not even where inner
life is concerned. And now, Laura was using this same
strategy to shape her subjectivity. I felt kinda used for
having had my birthday transformed into a way for her
to expand her network. When I accused her of this trick,
Laura was immediately offended at the insinuation that
she wouldn't have the clout to bring that core of people
together for her own sake, without needing some pre-
text. Then she appeared shocked that I could doubt her
goodwill, it truly was a gift of love, and you know, her
reaction did sound genuine, a mix of innocence and
cynicism. At first, that seemed an odd combination,
the union of two opposites, but thinking about it, it
made perfect sense as the consequence of an excessive

internalization, to the point where she could no longer tell what was rational, imposed, or true.

Acting happens both outward and inward. The performance is eternal, all the time, 24-7, throughout your life, an extended version of the Lee Strasberg method. You've got to remain alert, a moment's inattentiveness is all it takes, and then it's: Where's the emotion you're meant to be feeling, why isn't your grief convincing, where have your tears gone? On the outside, there are the rituals, the sharing of customs and codes, of habits and values—it's great to belong, it gives you a warm and fuzzy feeling in your heart, and that's independent of social class, it's as true in a village of four hundred as it is at a dinner *avec placement*. On the inside, there are our everyday ravings, the justification for our uglier actions, the conviction that we really are virtuous. If we're lucky, those around us confirm this impression, with a well-practiced choreography: the success of one person's performance depends on another's collaborating. If we're caught dancing samba while everyone else is doing ballet, there's this strangeness, there are all those doubts about whether our steps are right, confronting movements we're not sure about, and it's uncomfortable, best to go back to our partner.

Before the guests had sung "Happy Birthday," João Silva messaged to say he was at a party hosted by a gallery owner: *Boring crowd, but there's booze and drugs.*

Come over, and then we'll go on somewhere else, maybe downtown. I was dying of curiosity to see that house in person, I'd seen it in magazines, the collection looked stunning. Laura was confused when I decided to leave my own party. At least wait for the cake, she said, and I complied; impatiently, I quickly blew out the candles, downed my Negroni, and took a bottle of beer to drink in the cab. When I arrived, I saw there was security at the door—my name wasn't on the list, but I knew they wouldn't keep me out, even in my casual clothes, a simple black dress, just linen, with plain flat sandals, small earrings, because I'm white, I look like a rich person, I don't need a passport, the codes are genetic. I could have arrived carrying a plastic bottle with the leftover Negroni, the swimming-pool blue label still on it, half-full of red liquid, the thin slice of orange peel coming apart, kind of disgusting actually, my hands a bit slimy, and that wouldn't be seen as a failing, but rather the height of worldliness, the ultimate naturalness, 'cause I was born to be there. Sorry, could you toss this in the trash for me, please? I'd ask the security guard, smiling, polite, saying quietly: Thanks so much.

Pleasure comes in those moments when I feel invincible even without artificial stimulants. In the garden, all the women are in heels, except me. Better that way, as I can present an image of carefreeness. I discuss the political situation with a philosophy professor,

who praises my amusing insights. The head curator of
the New York museum joins us, and says: Oh yeah,
Vivian's awesome! And I delight in being there, in that
modernist house, drinking English gin with people I
think are important, just the same way my dad would
delight in being with some minister or other in Uncle Alberto's living room. At times like these, despite
impressing my interlocutors with the numbers I know
by heart relating to the exponential increase in political
violence in the country, I don't even remember Darlene.

It's good for me, and for my self-image, to think my
values go in the opposite direction to my parents'. They
save money so they can keep their address in the city's
prime location; I like living above a department store, in
the middle of a bustling avenue, right on all the bus routes
and next to the metro station, where I can buy drinks
from the street vendors all night long. To me, that's
practical, vibrant, rewarding. There's nothing more boring than a row of apartment blocks with their identical
verandas and their uniformed doormen, night and day.
It's not just an ethical problem, it's an aesthetic one,
mostly. Every day I learn to stop coming across as a rich
girl. I've got friends of all kinds and colors, I can move
around every corner of the city, self-assured, always natural, never arrogant. I mean, I'm not an idiot, I know it's
more about intangible capitalization than about virtue.
Nobody wants to be the dumbass who goes to the favela

and poses for a photo in front of the stall with their arm
around the flip-flop seller and then posts it on social media with a comment that's amusing, and fundamentally
offensive. Today, at least in the universe I inhabit, my
gay friends have more market value than the influencer
heiress. Maybe I'm just a brilliant strategist who's managed to dribble her way through her difficulties to turn
right around and come back to where she started. Any-
time I want, I can always go back to frequenting the
Noronha bourgeoisie with all the aristo pretensions,
and do this without any loss of status, or even with
some benefit, some exoticism, some interestingness. I
willingly accept Dad's offer to lend me his Sergio Rodrigues chair, I leave it on show in the living room, I or-
ganize more parties at home, and everyone knows what
that costs. I hate myself for it. But I can't stop.

I don't know if it's possible to live in an environment where there are no codes, where you can live
naked, outside any layers of representation. Now, I'm
drinking my eighth glass of champagne at the house of
some art collector who will certainly be amused at my
inappropriate remarks, impressed by my credentials.
Did you know I write for the *Frieze* site? The guy's
got money already, what he wants is to be able to go
up to his business partner, that totally underqualified
guy who only ever wants to spend his vacations at re-
sorts, and say: Oh, I'm a good friend of the artist's, of

the writer's, of the musician's. Unlike Laura, this guy doesn't even have any qualms about describing his latest investment, the painting by that artist with leukemia, can you imagine, it's gonna double in value soon enough. Next to this lack of decorum, any other person sounds discreet and civilized, just like the way we laugh at caricatured racists in American movies, with their aggressive comments, so inelegant and impassioned, and we can feel at peace for not being like them. Still, fuck it. I just want alcohol, the artist just wants to sell a piece of work, the curator just wants to look after the private collection, and this nouveau riche guy just needs a bit of guidance, poor bastard. At first, we ridicule someone like that, then right away we accept him among us— it's so easy to buy sophistication, you just need to stay alert.

9

Rodrigo and I have had this private ritual ever since we reconnected, after college. In the winter, we choose some beach to spend a week at, each of us with our own space, spending hours talking or hours in silence. Sometimes we go down to his family's place on the Rio–São Paulo border, close to Paraty. It's a four-hour drive, always to the same soundtrack, climaxing with Elis Regina's "Como Nossos Pais." At that moment, we sing together, the tears flow, then we play the track over again, twice, three times. Normally we choose a date when the cook is on vacation, because no mood of intimacy can survive a uniformed maid serving your breakfast, cleaning the living-room floor of the dirty little footprints that mark their territory as if to declare, blasé: Oh, we went to the beach, had a swim in the pool, ran across the grass, and came in here to fetch something, who cares? No, it's just awkward. We're in the twenty-first century, people don't have slaves any more, at least not in domestic homes. At the end of the week, we always regret our decision, we can't possibly clean that huge kitchen all on our own, it's practically the size of my apartment. I don't know why, but there was never enough time to wash all the dishes, there would always be a handful of dirty glasses and dishes left in the sink, sometimes spread around the house, in the dining room, in the bedroom, in the garden.

There's no such thing as a rich person who is genuinely good. Quite pleasant at most, Alex said before he learned anything about my family. I'd totally be a Robespierre type if I could, but I'm really more of a Marie Antoinette. Sometimes, I ask myself if I'm not a hypocrite, if I should do something more real, trade in my talk for concrete action, donate money to some movement, only there's never enough funds for things like that. In my defense, my bank account is always overdrawn, and every month my mom rescues me, otherwise my power gets cut off. But last week I did buy that little Jacquemus purse, seven hundred euro. I could have used that money for something else. Which would be a more coherent, humbler position to take, but also less fun, it would require a kind of sacrifice, and what for exactly? I have no idea how the money would get spent in a shelter. Who's to say it would even help the people who need it?

Maybe I'm just classist. I don't know if I'm smart enough to deserve my moderate professional success, I do read the odd book sometimes, but that's all, I'm kind of lazy, honestly. My main quality is my ability to accept a fair number of unpaid jobs that you need for an impeccable résumé. I don't have to pay rent or bills, or cover the costs of my phone and food; my earnings go to dinners, clothes, trips, alcohol, drugs. If I'm short of money, I cut out those latter things, feel like I'm making a sacrifice, investing in my career, two weekends staying in, I swap white cocaine for the yellow stuff. My family connections were strong enough to land me an internship at Inhotim during my college break, and from there every door opened, you just have to not be super dumb. But why, if I know all this, do I insist on wanting to be special?

If equality of conditions truly existed, would there be somebody else in my place with something more urgent to say? Could Darlene carry out these roles if she had the time and the education? Maybe then I'd have to give up my own position of relative distinction to take on a job that was banal. But I don't want to be insignificant to external eyes. I don't want to surrender my days to a job that's tedious. I don't want these issues to be made apparent. It's uncomfortable, tiresome. I want my advantages without also having to deal with the burden of watching some girl getting beaten up for no reason. If Darlene didn't exist, I could go on with my life. I'd go on thinking of myself as a good person.

I must, at all costs, maintain the self-image I have constructed, a person committed to certain causes, concerned for the community, for marginalized groups, the product of a structure that I'm part of and that I benefit from. It's my greatest commitment, I am what I think of myself. And reality can contradict me, that does happen sometimes, revealing unknown layers of my personality to myself and the world, layers that might not be very flattering, and I'll get a shock, and think: That's me, not cool, a bit selfish, kind of a jerk? I'm like a business that's maybe done some illegal stuff, there's no way the top brass can know everything that goes on, especially when you're talking about outsourced labor, we're not responsible, we have a statement on the subject, which our team has put together.

I do actually feel bad about it sometimes, but it soon passes, almost everybody around me is kind of the same. There's no real desire for social equality among the artistic class who studied in leftist constructivist schools. Nobody wants to admit that they might not have the talent to occupy a given prominent position. No, it's obvious they must all be great artists, committed to their jobs, just like their neighbors, schoolmates, childhood friends, second cousins, who are also prominent on the cultural scene. Quite the coincidence. They *surely* aren't a group of people with more contacts than substance. They aren't all inheritors of cultural or financial capital. They aren't the nobility. Everybody sees their own self-expression as relevant. They are moved by their own subjectivity, they're special, they're not bourgeois. Sure, often enough, the work might actually be well-done, quite correct, with all the necessary theoretical terminology, they sure got the education for it. João Silva always says: A person from the Zona Sul feels like they can call themselves an artist even when they're producing any old crap. In the Zona Norte, the condition's always subject to negotiation, something that's got to be won all the time and never gets entirely settled.

Basically our whole generation did a three-month study abroad in London or some such. When a friend disappears completely from the social scene on account of he's in rehab, that's the excuse we give: He's out of the country studying abroad. It's perfect, nobody gets suspicious, they're so used to it. Then, for the first time, it was true. Rodrigo went to New York to study sound engineering, he ran one course into the next, he kept staying on, it was meant to be three months and ended up being almost a year, and when he came back he was a performance artist, focusing on sound installations, and no longer a DJ: Because I'm never gonna feel complete if I got to depend on the approval of some crowd, at the end of the day electronic music maybe doesn't get played on the radio, but it's still commercial. Rodrigo spends a lot of money trying to prevent his identity from being based on money. In the past, he'd been renting this three-bed apartment right on Leblon beach. But he didn't like seeing his mother's friends insulting the supermarket cashier, better just to break the lease, find someplace in a less ostentatious neighborhood, with the appropriate furniture, which suited his new life plan. That way he could be seen as a person who was committed to something greater than the petty sticklers of that provincial high society. His solution was to buy a place in the old workers' housing at Horto, in Jardim Botânico.

The area's way more charming than that oppressive vibe you get in Leblon, he says. There's nothing too showy, no expensive restaurants, none of those ill-mannered ladies flouncing down the sidewalks clutching their designer purses, with suspicious glances from side to side, always alert, ready to cross over to the other sidewalk, 'cause you never know when they might appear, just ten meters from you, one of those dangerous *black* children. On the contrary, the social mix here is healthy, with moneyed artists as next-door neighbors to the original employees of the old cotton factory. Obviously, the new residents' homes have all been done up, fitted with Brazilian designer furniture and pieces of contemporary art, all of this more in tune with the adjusted prices of the only bakery on the street, which now sells three different brands of alfajor. There are subtle differences between the facades, too, the surviving workers aren't allowed to make major structural changes because of the cultural heritage regulations. To begin with, the ground level of the house was occupied by João Silva—he had no money and a friend sublet her old studio to him cheaply while he was overdrawn. The idea was that he'd stay till she returned from her residency abroad, which was set to last around a year. It was enough space, about 100 square meters, a yard with trees and a hammock, and he never ran into the neighbors who rented the second and third floors, none of them with leases. In the first month, Rodrigo went to João Silva's intending, perhaps, to buy a picture, and he fell in love with the possibility of transforming that simple building, with its cheap finishes, poor-quality materials, into a more comfortable home, a mini townhouse. He immediately made the owner a generous offer, before calling in a good architect and knocking through the walls of the kitchen, which now opens into the living room, which does make gatherings of friends feel more intimate. To this day, he has no idea his little workers' house is on the preservation register. João Silva found someplace else, more expensive and farther away; as for the upstairs neighbors, I've got no clue about them.

Since the move, Rodrigo has gotten more and more interested in politics, even attending meetings with candidates for deputies, where they put forward their proposals for culture. He got excited and offered his house as the stage for the next debate, and that way he could even invite his parents, who collect art and are gold patrons of MASP. I thought it best to warn him: Rodrigo, these guys aren't stupid. You know they're gonna be laughing at your parents behind their back, they'll end up a joke. But I might have overestimated Horto's artist class. Or maybe, encouraged by the surname that is the name of a bank, not knowing that they were dealing with the black sheep, who might end up getting disinherited entirely, they actually believed his fanciful plans of setting up a publishing house, an art gallery, a movie production company.

Right away, Rodrigo was included in every gathering, and spurred by this new belonging, which created good opportunities for work and for sex, he began to make his own first acquisitions, even finally buying his first João Silva. In six months, he was producing the soundtrack to a movie, he'd started a romance with a cinema director, and his wall was covered with canvases and photographs, by young artists as well as established ones. As the economy got shakier, Rodrigo rose in importance. Everybody likes a patron, especially with the country on the verge of bankruptcy. Often enough, somebody complains: It's such a drag these days, with museums having all these quotas now for minorities, even if they're totally talentless. And Marina Falcão says: For God's sake, quotas have always been around, quotas for rich people, even if *they're* totally talentless, what difference does it make, at least it's a different kind of quota now, maybe something new might come of it, who knows. Everything passes from us, the heavens and the earth, cultural fads, the economic situation, the prevailing political ideology, everything except Rodrigo. He is our only hope, our redeemer.

10

For the last several months, outside my building, there have been other people selling beer, I don't know if these people alternate, one of them doing half the week and the other doing the other half, or if there's somebody permanent, the way I thought it was with Darlene. These days I prefer buying from the other side of the street, where theoretically an execution took place, according to what Darlene once told me. On the other side of the street they take credit and debit cards, outside my building it's cash only. Every night, when I'm heading out to a bar, a club, a party, a show, a dinner, a play, a museum, an exhibition, I take a good look down the sidewalk, left and right, before getting into my cab, to see if I might find Darlene. She's never there, or, I dunno, maybe she was there at some point, but I've had toxoplasmosis in my eyes, I don't see straight. When I'm having a party and I need to go downstairs to restock the fridge in the middle of the night, I never find her, and for a few moments I imagine the worst. Then I quickly come up with some excuse, like she must have swapped to a new spot. Somewhere Darlene's off selling her Heinekens in Copacabana, Ipanema, Gávea, Glória, Gamboa, Lapa, maybe farther away, apparently there's a lively scene in Baixo Méier. Sometimes I can't help feeling I think about this every day, someplace deep in my thoughts, and I even tell other people, referring to the events I witnessed, that it's a trauma, but I don't know if that's true. It's easy to sublimate traumatic events when they happen to someone else. Maybe I'm just indifferent, like I always was. And if I'm really honest, I know that I don't very much care if Darlene is alive or dead.

In December, I learned almost accidentally of her death. I was on the other side of the street, buying beer on my debit card, the machine wasn't working, the whole process was taking forever, and I'd already opened the bottle. I was getting impatient with the seller, he was embarrassed, the minutes were dragging, and for some reason I asked: Hey, and what's the deal with Darlene, who used to sell beer out here, where's she at these days? The reply was in the joyless half smile that formed on that man's lips, kind of sad-looking. She died. At home, head trauma, he said. I immediately regretted the question. What was I supposed to feel:

grief, guilt, indifference, sadness? It was like I'd entered a new environment whose codes I didn't properly know, and I was supposed to understand, intuitively, how to behave and act in the moment, based on that understanding. They ought to teach us some kind of emotional etiquette.

I don't feel "survivor's guilt," it wouldn't be right to use that term, my own existence was always assured, I was never in danger. And if something did happen to me, well, it'd be a shame, a life cut short, so young, so many dreams, this city is under siege, you can't even walk the streets anymore. The person who died isn't from my family, from my group, it's almost like she was from some other country, some other land, other values, another language, like a chemical attack in Damascus. And however much there might be something being forged inside me that's maybe a little bit like guilt, it's only there for the purposes of self-congratulation. It's a shapeless feeling, and I'm able to control its intensity, choose what fills its vacuum, borrow another's pain, write about empathy.

I've got very little understanding of the weight of the world. I don't know hunger, I don't know death, I don't know love. My existence is a search for small victories that sound important at the time. So I desire smaller victories still, like I am walking around scanning the ground with my eyes for coins. They're small wins, more concrete than a sort of intangible sense of fulfillment, which doesn't last long at all, its consistency is fragile, too abstract, easily lost in your memory. Even the most vivid sensation in the world has so many layers and subtleties that it can be questioned even by the person who actually felt it. Is it love or neediness, generosity or narcissism, a soulmate connection or just the psychedelic effects of ayahuasca? While small wins are verifiable, they don't run the risk of being mistaken for a mere impression, maybe an illusion. Their appearance is superficial, comfortable, pleasurable, there's a security in that.

The melancholy that I feel isn't existential, but selfish. It's a deep suffering in the soul at not having won enough victories to put me on a stable footing. This distress tormenting me doesn't happen because I'm afraid of hunger or death, but because I want to be sexier, more sought-after, more successful. It's not conscious, they're desires that appear in moments of weakness, when I'm distracted. Like the instrumental music at a bar, you don't notice how bad it is because you're talking loud, worried about pleasing other people, securing that night's small victory. There are few things uglier than a bar when the lights come on after the last customer's been kicked out. The décor wasn't made for white light, the upholstery's covered in stains, the smell of cigarettes is nauseating, there's probably a body behind the sofa, asleep, covered in their own vomit, abandoned by their friends. That's why I always want to keep the lights low.

When I picture the perfect scenario for finding a kind of peaceful contentment, I always add something else, at the last minute, as if I was at the drugstore, my basket already holding everything I need, standing in front of the hair-care products, and thinking: Why don't I buy one more, just a pack of elastics, a shower comb, it's all so cheap, won't make any difference. Before I know it I'm home with a plastic bag full of assorted little bits of paraphernalia. And even so, even if I do feel fulfilled, content, at peace, my life is still incomplete, it doesn't matter, even if there's comfort and love, and everything's okay, the thought assails me, the sight of myself through someone else's eyes, someone who hurt me in the past, and I can tell that just being peaceful's not enough, I need to shine. Albertinho needs to apologize to me, not out of any genuine remorse, but because I have the power to damage his reputation. The satisfaction isn't photogenic, it's not connected to success, so it's a valid question: Is this really what I want? I don't know if silent, anonymous happiness is enough for my desires.

If Beckett hadn't been such an iconic writer, people wouldn't keep repeating that line of his about failing so often. If he was just some regular encyclopedia salesman, his speech would just be defeatist. Nobody giving a commencement address ever quotes a line about the

importance of failure that was said by anyone who actually failed. Something like: My uncle always wanted
to be an artist, he spent his whole life working in public
office, his only exhibition didn't sell one single misera-
ble picture, the local paper considered his work lacking
in expressiveness. And on his deathbed, in debt, abandoned by his family, in a house full of old furniture and
power outages, he shared this lesson: There is no better
teacher than failure. It's not the destination that matters, it's the journey. Happiness is in the little things.
No, those speeches always come out of the mouths of
billionaires who see themselves as oh-so-wise and who
love giving advice about the mysteries of life.

Knowing who I am from the outside is as hard as
knowing who I am from the inside. Memory mixes
them up, which makes everything even more confus-
ing. Does the Vivian who existed in the world ten years
ago, with her specific choices, get transformed into the
inside Vivian when she becomes a memory? In other
words, does time ingest the past exterior me, to then
incorporate it into the interior me of the present? Is
what I'm saying obvious? If I'm at a party, surrounded
by friends, drinking a Negroni, do I look alone? I don't
care about the image I've got on social media, I care
about that exact moment of suspension when I'm not
talking to anybody. Cocaine supplies those empty
spaces with a ready-made persona, takes away any

individualization—everyone ends up in the same pro-
tected pose. That's the fun part, the illusion that your
soul is armored—it isn't, not ever, but we believe it for
those few hours. Sometimes, for some reason, I realize
I'm sober, the packed bar doesn't help, it's this whole
huge saga to get your hands on a drink, every attempt
to get served is a serious test of your patience. In those
moments I know that the look in my eyes is lost, vulnerable, out of place. It's like that eighteen-year-old girl
who had never been kissed on the mouth was curiously
watching all that bustle of people through my eyes, not
knowing how to react. Bit by bit, she occupies more
and more space in my body and soul, until the eyes
aren't mine, but hers.

I want to kill that girl. I could repress her, but I'm
sure that would only come back on me as insecurity, the
symptoms teeming uncontrollably until I'm behaving
just like those people I judge and criticize. I could re-
frame the story to make it sound like a journey of overcoming. As I enumerate the specific achievements I'm
proud of, and which will allow me, little by little, and with
great effort, to kill that girl, I reveal a certain libertar-
ian fascination, and I go back to being her. There's no
way out. Vivian, the Catholic virgin about to start college, always manages to resurface, one way or another,
and there's no exorcism that can fix that. On those rare
nights when my feelings about my journey are proud

and loving, I can transform that shame into affection. There's a purity in that fascination that doesn't get talked about much—it's childish, naive, almost sweet.

I want everything, I want glamour, I want sex, I want to party, I want beautiful clothes, I want to re-model my apartment, I want peace, I want to help people, I want true love, I want the admiration of my friends, but also of acquaintances, people I say "Hey, how's it going?" to. I want a clear conscience, I want to be respected for my character and for my persona, I don't want to lie, not to myself or anyone else. Maybe I'm a curator of myself, I select the very best experi-ences, then get the word out: going out to some cheap little bar in the favela, using drugs, that ménage with two girls last Carnaval, my three Black friends, who show up in every photo I post online. I'm not a frag-mented, contradictory person, at once good and bad, I am one, I'm coherent, hermetic, a rounded, realis-tic character who produces some empathy, guaran-tees some entertainment. It's like every aspect of my life gained meaning only after being appropriately molded. You're not suffering from depression, Marina's always telling me, you're suffering from internalized capitalism.

As an adolescent, my Catholic and volunteer groups were my only contacts with the little beautiful people. The few fifteenth birthday parties I got invited to were through Confirmation classes. The teachers, who were friends of my mom's, were always going on about overcoming adversity through faith. Personally, I was quite committed to this, because I was in serious need of God's help. And so I studied, I sought out further reading, suggested topics for discussion. My favorite subjects were not welcome. Since we're organizing the end-of-year charity bazaar, I once suggested, maybe it'd be interesting to read the parable of the poor widow. It's in Luke 21? All this caused some controversy and discomfort. Even there, I wasn't much loved. The bathrooms were very cold at the sanctuary of Lourdes, in the Pyrenees. If I prayed, maybe I'd stop being so lonely, maybe I'd start getting invited to parties, maybe I'd be included in that select group, and I wouldn't cry so much. Anything to be cured.

It's in the Bible—"Blessed are those who hunger and thirst for righteousness"—but you may as well forget it, that part doesn't matter. God created the little pink impatiens and He created the imperial palms. Wishing for an end to world hunger is a cliché, the sort of thing you'd expect from a beauty pageant contestant. This conformity is internalized, way back in childhood, as second nature. In theory, ignoring these questions should require some effort, but no. Just outside the front door there's a guy on the verge of starvation, practically part of the landscape. It's not an issue, we don't even think about it: What's it like sleeping on the street, what happens when it rains, I wonder if there's rats, I wonder if they get murdered, I wonder if they get used to the dirt? I wonder if they're different from us, who want to puke when we're pulling our own hair out of the bathtub drain? I wonder if they're immune to disgust?

Financial and social inheritance brings, along with all its perks, a subtle psychological cost, an original sin. The Bible also says that he who is given most will have most required of him. Will they discount the ten years of depression I had in my school days? Or maybe I still need to pay for the sins of my parents, their choices that seem alternately shameful and interesting. The world should make Darlene's existence easier, not make mine worse. I've already got to deal with distress, anxiety, depression. Deep down, all I want is for the woman not to get beaten up while she's working her shift, right in front of me.

It was 4 a.m., I was in that square, in the middle of the dance floor, kissing two guys at the same time. Darlene was the one who was at the police station, in the hospital, then crying at home, maybe just resigned to it—I don't know where you even go after something like that, don't know what it's like to experience that sort of treatment as routine, it's all alien to me. Most likely Darlene lived in the favela, or otherwise out in the suburbs, but maybe she was married to a cab driver and they lived together in a one-bed in Copacabana. I don't know what the monthly income of a beer seller is, or of a cab driver, but no matter. Do I really need to watch that scene that stops me fulfilling my part in the social contract? If a tree falls in an empty forest, maybe it doesn't make a sound, maybe it didn't even fall, maybe it never even existed. But if I witness the tree falling, I'll have to deal with it differently. I'll read the paper, produce the usual performative indignation, which actually is true and brings me satisfaction, because it reassures me that I'm not a sociopath, but it'll last only five minutes.

Whenever I develop some plan to escape from this moral inertia, I think: What's the point? The structures are still intact, it's all just rearranging the deck chairs, liberal activism, change through consumption, it's basically just a couple of steps from there to the logic of charity, making some big speech à la Mimi de la Blétière. What could I actually do to change Darlene's situation? Give her a hundred reais, a car, a health-care plan? Pay for her son's doctor, get her brother-in-law a job, help her community, make a movie? Darlene, the movie, Darlene, the main character, Darlene, the actress, I mean, not Darlene herself, who's dead, but somebody like her. Vivian Noronha, director, screenwriter, producer—you never know, I might win an

Oscar, a Tony, the Nobel. In that way my public re-
demption will be applauded, I'll be redeemed—no,
more than that, canonized. Maybe that's my destiny. I
owe Darlene all my strength and commitment to make
this happen. And I'll be grateful, I'll find out what her
surname was, and it will be printed on all the posters
as the woman who saved me. Thank you, Darlene, I
say now, and I'll say next week, next month, next year,
when I'm up on that stage, receiving some award. I
won't forget you. I'll say: Thank you, Darlene. My hair
up, a high topknot, with a few strands loose, suitably
brushed, understated lipstick, a natural color, some
light shadowing on the eyes, lilac dress, something
square-necklined and simple, though maybe the back
could be bare, down to the waist. And in that movie
I'd include an idealized version of myself, there'd be no
cheap moralizing as compensation, it would be a quiet
sort of integrity, no fanfare, which other people would
realize gradually, and then they'd say: Vivian, you're
the best person I know.

There's a degree of sociopathy in going on living
while Darlene is dead—Darlene isn't Darlene, obviously,
Darlene never was Darlene, she's just a reminder of the
world, she's inside of me. Still, I keep going, to honor
her memory, to change careers, write a story, attain
success. I want to be honored, I want to receive hon-
ors. And now, suddenly, the movie's not about her, it's

about me, and I insert an idealized version of myself as a character, gripped by the idea of reconstructing myself, in a literal sense now. On the night Darlene died, I was smoking a cigarette and holding a brandy, alone on the streets of Copacabana. In my memory of that night, I'm thinner, more beautiful—the actress who's cast is always a physically better version—hair all billowy, dress like a nightie, all lacy and red, with black combat boots, a Marina Lima song playing on Avenida Atlântica. The one thing you can get from me: solitude with a view of the sea.

Nobody thinks of themselves as superficial, and maybe no one really is, maybe human depth is uniform, like how the arrangement of our internal organs is uniform, maybe it's just in the workings that's there's a difference. Not that that's relevant—I could die without having made contact with other dimensions of myself. What happens to unrevealed feelings after a person dies? The guilt isn't for Darlene—she's just the most visible aspect of it, practically a metaphor, poor thing, even after her death she's still stripped of importance. The guilt is for the suspicion that maybe I'd be happy if I'd ignored the external pressures I did always think were so insignificant. They're all so small that it's embarrassing to think I care so much, that I've devoted so many hours of my life to minor materialistic paranoias. Now I'm confronted with just the opposite feeling, the naivete of looking for something related to the spirit, to invisible qualities, honestly I might as well believe in angels. But if that's the case, if the incorporeal dimension of the world doesn't matter, then what is this hole in my chest? Is it hunger, is it colic, a lack of serotonin?

If I think about Darlene as a real human being, my heart explodes. It's only people I know who are human beings, or alternatively celebrities, public figures, 'cause I do get sad if they die, even if only briefly, sometimes I even cry. There are other living beings too, like pets, like my dog who lives at my parents' house—he's like a sibling to me, even more so than Laura. Fetuses, however, aren't human beings, so long as they're still inside the belly. They're not human beings even if they're several months old, 'cause if society sees them like that, then I lose rights over my body. I'm a woman, not a reproducing machine, or a second-class citizen. Moralists will say that I'm the one who's inhuman for saying these things, that I'm cruel, but they're wrong—I am a human being, the same species that's been here for millennia, not a saint, not divine, but earthly, I'm what there is. It's horrible, I know, but that's the world, and I'm in the world. And when I say that, I'm filled with a sense of grandeur, the beauty of being part of something bigger, even if that something is rotten.

In December, I spent a few days feeling unsettled, thinking about the information I'd received, a

week earlier, about Darlene's fate. For the first time, I
snorted coke on my own, 6 p.m., dark glasses, by the
window, then I lit a cigarette, opened a beer, looked
at myself in the mirror and felt beautiful, deep, com-
plex, sexy. In that moment, I considered messaging the
museum designer, inviting him over for a session of
snorting and fucking—after all, there was every reason to believe he'd be receptive, given his personality,
our history of flirting, and even, in the small hours
of one Sunday morning, an exchange of nudes. Very
likely I'd find him in some dirty old bar getting wasted,
shirtless, brown hair in curls, tousled, still unshaven,
charming and kinda crazy. Maybe that wasn't a good
idea—just imagine the hangover, the yellow coke, cheap
alcohol, meaningless sluttery, and Darlene's ghost. Better to go back home, take a cold shower, wash my hair,
turn on the AC, make myself a caprese salad, open a
bottle of nicely chilled white wine, and call Luiz Felipe. We hadn't talked in, what, about ten months? In
which time he'd gotten himself a girlfriend, some yoga
teacher, vegetarian, mandala tattoo, and together they,
the perfect couple, took a cycling trip down the Andes,
I think? Apparently they've broken up now, I dunno,
but in any case he agreed to come over, said he'd leave
home in half an hour.

    In the bedroom, I put the red bulb in the lamp,
connected my phone to the speaker, chose some playlist

or other, something foolproof I'd used before. My expectation was that we'd fuck for five, six, seven hours, like we had in the past, and that he'd curse me out, choke me, hit me, even more intensely—god, I'm so controlling, so programmed, so rational that I even planned the catharsis, the exorcism, the release. I could go to church, to the Spiritist house, to a terreiro, to a meditation retreat, to a psychoanalyst, but frankly this way's more pleasurable, shock therapy, mainlined straight to the unconscious.

Luiz Felipe was still totally hot, and he didn't ask much, apparently he didn't notice anything out of the ordinary, maybe there wasn't time, so I put the bottle of wine down onto the table, unbuttoned his pants, started sucking him, slowly, carefully, attentively, the best blow job in the world, and soon we were in bed, following all the usual rituals, the slapping, the fisting, the cursing, the little rape fantasy, the double penetration. At that point, it made no sense for me to say unsex me here because I was being penetrated hard, and when he turned me over for the first time I felt pain, like this was too violent for my ass, like I was being ripped apart, but I didn't complain, and I think he mistook my cry of pain for pleasure, especially after I said: Don't stop. No idea why I said that, the words just appeared suddenly like a surprise, came out of my mouth, and I started to cry. On the table was the black bow I'd previously had around my neck, now undone into a simple strip of fabric; I reached out my hand to take it and gestured vaguely with it to attract Luiz Felipe's attention. The movement was understood in the light of our previous encounters, in the way, perhaps, that I wanted. He held my two fists so firmly together that my arms felt inanimate. Then he used the ribbon to immobilize my body. Sex fulfills the same function as dreaming, it reveals who we are through encrypted language—but we hardly ever remember our dreams. I don't know how I'd even have sex if my mom hadn't aborted my youthful attempts at masturbation. I need to be reborn, to wash away my sins, be part of a ritual, receive a passing-over of hands, drink ayahuasca, kill my father. And, once again, I try to rationalize it away, basic like in some first-semester class, something I read online, a PDF somebody sent me, a conversation with João Silva. And I think about Darlene. If I could go back in time, I'd do something to protect her. I could have saved Darlene, she'd still be alive. And I could tell people the story as proof of my virtue. But no, I moved away, the party looked promising, for a moment I was scared the police might find my drugs, that they'd be annoyed at my interfering, even though, let's face it, worst-case scenario it would still be no more than an inconvenience, my dad's friends with the governor, the guy's constantly around our place. At that point, barely conscious, I get spat at in my face and I say: Don't stop. It seems almost surreal when he kisses me on the mouth. My face must be red, all that crying. And once again, Darlene, not her, but her family, who I don't know, I'm just imagining them, her mom would still be alive, living in the same house, she'd take care of her younger sisters, maybe a husband, a stonemason, a doorman, a street sweeper. The family of the poor murdered woman is dealing with mourning, distress, hardships, but it's all right, some clouds have a silver lining—I wouldn't have done all this thinking, and transformed myself, if the police hadn't murdered Darlene. And so I understand my place in the world. In some way, I believe my mom's narrative that we aren't rich, and I have the same fear of scarcity, which I can rationalize as ridiculous, but I share it. Luiz Felipe's being lazy about this oral sex—it's only the third time he's gone down on me, and we've been here so many hours. I'm fifteen, I'm on my way to school with the driver, sitting in the back seat. At the time, we had three cars, the everyday one, the one for trips, and the one for the dogs, which was the only one not armored. I get out of the car, in my pleated Catholic school skirt and navy sweater, and one of the boys at the gate curses me out; I try to keep looking straight ahead, walk down the hall without looking at the group, when one of them spits out his gum on the floor and I get a start. I thought I'd be the target, but I wasn't—he was the only boy who was nicer, who never got involved in that sort of messing about. Still, I get startled, and I stop walking for a minute, and I see that the boy got startled too, there's a connection between us, something in his eyes calms me. At some after-party, 5 a.m., a group of people I know is having fun bad-mouthing me, it's normal, I do it to other people, why wouldn't they do it to me? And now, I'm naked yet dressed, under the red light, the shadows of the blinds disguising my stretch marks, so that I'm beautiful, unquestionably beautiful, like in my best photograph. Luiz Felipe is looking at my face, he smiles, replaces "you little slut" with a "you're really lovely." I didn't want him to alter the dynamics, to change tone, and I don't want to give anything away, and it's late, the black ribbon is on the floor, my neck gets a kiss, my breasts a caress. I run my hand down my body, and when I arrive between my legs everything feels too wet, at first I think it's cum, maybe he ejaculated, that does happen sometimes, but it's different, there's something else. I keep on running back up my stomach, chest, bring my hand to my face, and in the half-light I can see something dark, my hand, the sheet, everything's covered in blood. Luiz Felipe looks at me. And at once he smiles, serene: Oh, you're on your period? I didn't know you were on your period.

ACKNOWLEDGMENTS

My friends are my family, and I want to thank them for being by my side during the writing of this book, helping me with critical readings of the manuscript or with emotional support, or simply existing: Alice Galeffi, Beatriz Sonoda Falcão, Bernardo de Souza, Bettina Birmarcker, Camila Regis, Claudio Seichi Kawakami Savaget, Daniel Morais, Gabriel Raggio, Gabriel Ribeiro, Juliana Cunha, Luana Moussallem, Luiza Calmon, Luiza Vianna, Matheus Rocha Pitta, Matilde Azevedo Neves, Tomás Toledo, Victor Gorgulho, Zé Ortigão. And, naturally, none of this would have been possible without the care and attention of my amazing editor, Emilio Fraia, and of my wonderful agent, Marianna Teixeira Soares.